AN UNCONVENTIONAL MOURNING

SAM CHEEVER

ELECTRIC PROSE PUBLICATIONS

~

What could be more entertaining than a professional mourner's convention? An actually dead actor lying in a prop coffin. And a heroine who realizes if she doesn't find the killer fast, somebody else is going to die. Namely her.

MayBell is excited to attend her very first Professional Mourner's convention. She's looking forward to meeting other mourners and picking up tips to improve her graveside performances. Anticipating days filled with representative mourning situations and training, May quickly discovers that the corpse lying in the coffin is all too real. To make things worse, May appears to be the last person to have seen the victim the night before.

May quickly finds herself on the hot seat to find a killer. There are just a couple of small problems. First, her suspect pool includes over a hundred professional mourners and vendors. And second, the real killer doesn't want May to discover the truth. Making her unusual mourning situation not only tricky but unconventionally deadly as well.

STAY IN TOUCH

1

"How dare you!"

Shoving my long, dark-gold hair behind an ear, I jerked to a halt and looked around, my ever-ready sense of guilt flaring at the angry words. Down by my feet, my Pomeranian companion, Shakespeare, gave a soft yip and tucked his fanlike tail.

There was nobody in the hallway with us. Even the potted palms, my personal favorite spot for hiding, were too small to hide the speaker.

Another voice rumbled in response to the first and I realized someone was having an argument around the corner...near the elevators that were my intended destination.

"I certainly did not! Why must you always accuse me..."

The woman's voice cut off as she likely listened to a response I couldn't hear.

The ding of the arriving elevator yanked me out of listening mode and into action. "Come on, buddy," I told my small but mighty companion. We hurried forward in the hopes of catching the elevator before the doors closed. I was already late for a lecture on understanding the characteristics of grief and the elevators in the ancient Mountain View Conference Center were notoriously slow. If I didn't catch the car, Shakes and I would have to hoof it quickly down four flights of stairs.

The whir of the doors closing spurred me into a run. "Can you hold the doors please?" We whipped around the corner and I groaned as I realized I was too late. The elevator dinged its descent toward floor number four.

Shakes started to bark, his tiny body pinging off the carpet with each woof. A figure stood before a small couch, a notebook in his hand and a scowl on his attractive face. He hurried past us, murmuring in a deep, husky voice. "Excuse me."

I watched him stride quickly down the hallway for a beat and then turned toward the nearby stairwell. "Come on, buddy," I sighed. "We're going to have to take the stairs."

Diving into the stairwell, I put the incident of the argument behind me and focused on the fact that I was nearly ten minutes late for my first lecture. It was a heck of a way to kick off my first professional mourner's convention.

Moments later, I slammed out of the stairwell as if my heels were on fire. Shakes and I ran across the lobby, the little dog's nails clicking a path across the glossy tile.

Reaching for the door to the lecture room, I halted at the sound of a familiar voice calling my name.

"May! Wait up, dolly!"

My head snapped around to find Pinella Gerrard, my eighty-year-old unmarried neighbor clacking her way toward me on a pair of shiny black kitten heels. I blinked at the unfortunate sight of the skin-tight onesie that matched the heels in both color and shininess stretched over her octogenarian-type body. "Pinella," I said, frowning. "What are you doing here?"

The elderly woman's heavily-lipsticked mouth curved and she winked. "I'm a paid actress now, dolly. Didn't you get my email?"

I *had* gotten an email from Pinella the night before. To say it was illegible would be a vast understatement. The note had read, "Se U 2m 4 cof death. Sew Xcite." Our neighbor Doug had taught Pinella all about texting, and she'd given it her own manic spin as she did most things. "I got an email from you at eleven PM. I was asleep, and you woke me up."

Thunderous clapping erupted inside the lecture room. I did an internal sigh. I was officially late.

"What were you doing up so late?" I asked my neighbor.

She flipped a dismissive hand. "I don't sleep much these days. Your perspective on the whole sleeping thing changes the older you get. All too soon, I'll be sleeping forever. Why waste the time I have?"

Though depressing, her attitude made a certain grim kind of sense. "Anyway," I said, smiling at her. "I have no idea what the text was supposed to say."

Pinella looked scandalized. "Dolly, you're too young to be text illiterate. You need to take a texting lesson from Doug."

I opened my mouth to tell her I didn't need a lesson with him and that his medical-marijuana-infused lessons had probably destroyed Pinella's ability to communicate in her native language forever, and then snapped it closed again. It was possible my crankiness at being late for my first lecture was coloring my mood just a titch. "Tell me again, in real English, what you're doing here."

"I'm getting paid to act like one of the stiffs in the coffins."

Well, that was plain speaking. "Oh." I wasn't sure how I felt about that. I wasn't excited to see Pinella lying in a coffin looking deceased. But I didn't want to talk about that with her because of the broad array of potential landmines stretching out before us. "Congratulations?"

She laughed. "Don't look so stricken, dolly. I'm not gonna be knockin' on Heaven's doors anytime soon. A little practice run won't hurt anything."

I winced. "I'll take your word on that." Secretly, I doubted Pinella would ever get that close to Heaven. I was thinking she'd probably end up in a cute little fire-retardant bungalow near the fiery-pits.

More clapping drifted from the room I was tardy entering.

"We're late. I need to get in there. Shouldn't you go in the back way?"

Pinella blew a raspberry. "That's a whole lot of walking, dolly. I'm going this way because it's the closest."

I didn't ask if she was sure. Though the question was dancing on the end of my tongue. I figured she knew her business. Surely the organizers had provided training for the coffin-rider gig.

I shrugged. "Okay. Let's go then. I just want to sneak quietly inside and sit in the back row. No fuss, no unwarranted attention. Got it?"

She nodded as if she understood. But it became painfully obvious as soon as we walked through the doors that she hadn't understood.

She hadn't understood at all.

Over a hundred people sat in the large ballroom on folding chairs. Over a hundred people turned from the speaker on the stage when Pinella and I walked into the room. Several gasps sounded throughout the room, probably because Pinella's outfit would have stood out on a much younger woman. On a woman her age, it engendered a distinct mix of shock and horror that was hard to ignore. She stood out like a pole dancer in a room full of nuns.

Even the speaker stared out at us, his face puckered with irritation.

As a taut silence pounded down on me, I gave in to the need to break the tension. "I'm sorry. There was an...elevator incident."

A low murmur started through the room, like the flight of a thousand angry hornets advancing on an encroaching enemy. I stared longingly at a lone empty seat in the farthest back row, probably left unfilled because of its nearness to a heavy velvet drape that half obscured its occupant.

I coveted that seat like an avid reader craves her next great book.

"Hello!" Pinella crooned, waving happily around the room. "I'm your friendly neighborhood corpse. If you'll just point me in the direction of my casket, I'll happily stretch out there for a little nap."

Titters sounded around the room. I eased toward the draperied chair. If I moved really slowly, the hundreds of gazes might not track my movement.

Of course, I could never be so lucky. "This is my friend, MayBell. She's a funeral faker like y'all. Isn't that fun?"

More than a hundred hostile gazes swung my way as if I'd been the one to utter the hated "funeral faker" phrase. I shook my head, a nervous laugh escaping before I could stop it. "She's just kidding." I glared over at Pinella. "She knows what we do is genuine theater and has an important place in the grieving process."

Pinella gave me an exaggerated wink. "Of course it is, dolly."

I fought the almost irrepressible desire to slink off to the half-hidden chair.

The speaker apparently decided it was time for him to step in and staunch the bleeding. "If you ladies wish to join the lecture, please take your seat...or coffin. You're putting us behind schedule."

I inclined my head, nodding toward the coffins arrayed along the base of the stage. "Go find an empty one and climb aboard," I said to my neighbor in a harsh whisper.

She gave me an arthritic thumbs up and clacked her way down the aisle toward the stage. Like storm watchers observing a particularly devastating category five hurricane, all eyes followed her swaying, clicking, occasionally hitching movements toward the stage.

I gratefully took the coveted half-draped chair and did my best to melt back into the curtains.

My peace and anonymity lasted only the amount of time it took for Pinella to find an empty coffin.

Her voice rang out loud and clear to once again interrupt the irate speaker. "Don't they have no stepstools for these things? Hey, dolly. Can you give me a boost? I don't wanta break a hip climbing this thing like a stripper pole."

I sank slowly into my chair and wished for invisibility.

To my vast chagrin. It never came.

2

"How's it going?" my boyfriend asked.

I groaned softly into the phone, looking around the restaurant to make sure nobody was sitting close enough to hear. "Don't ask. Pinella took a job as a coffin surfer."

Eddie barked out a laugh. "Coffin surfer?"

"It's what she calls it. Don't repeat that though. It might start a riot. She called us funeral fakers yesterday and I thought I might have to throw her over my shoulder and run."

He chuckled. "My lips are locked. So, what's she doing? Other than embarrassing you at every opportunity?"

"So much that. Yesterday I was late to my first lecture and I ran into her in the lobby. She insisted on coming into the ballroom with me and it plunged downward from there."

"I need details."

"Details? Here's a detail. At one point she was draped over the side of the coffin with her butt in the air and her skinny legs flailing as she tried to, as she put it, 'climb the coffin like she climbs Tommy the Toy at Hustler's strip club on the edge of town'."

"Such a visual." There was gasping from the other end of the line. "You're making that up."

"I wish. Picture me shoving her skinny buttocks trying to heave her over the top into the coffin. Two guys came out of the audience to help me and Pinella tried to get their phone numbers."

More gasping. "You're killin' me here."

I fought a smile. I supposed from a distance, the incident probably sounded pretty hilarious. It definitely hadn't been funny at the time. It had been humiliating. "Anyway. I'm thinking about donning a disguise for the rest of the convention. Maybe she won't recognize me."

"Good luck with that. How's the convention other than that? Have you learned anything useful?"

I never got a chance to respond. A shrill scream curdled on the air. I leaped up without thinking. "I have to go," I told Eddie. And then I was running, emerging from the restaurant into the lobby, which was much thicker than usual with people. The wide-open doors of the nearby lecture room explained why. The attendees who had previously filled the oversized room had all flooded into the lobby. Conversation was frantic and several people were in tears.

Through the open doors I could see an empty podium on a naked stage and, beside it on the floor, a toppled casket. From where I stood, a messy cap of silver-white hair was barely visible on the other side of the fallen coffin.

"No," I murmured. "Pinella!" I screamed. And then I was plunging through the gaping doors, struggling against a tide of oversized men who kept trying to grab me.

I dodged left and right, my frantic gaze locked on that messy cap of hair. Tears were already burning my eyes when

I slammed into a flesh-covered wall and my forward momentum was brutally halted.

"Hold on there, ma'am," the big man drawled. His height of well over six feet dwarfed my measly five feet nine inches. The man's brown eyes filled with pity. "Do you know the woman in that casket?"

I shook my head in silent denial. If I kept telling myself it couldn't be her, maybe it wouldn't be.

His slightly bulging brown gaze narrowed. "You need to stay outside, Miss. The police have been called. We need to keep the scene as pristine as possible."

I stood eye to pec with the man, so it was easy to read his name badge. I could tell by the taser on his duty belt and the radio he was clutching in his hand that he was hotel security. "Look, Dobson..."

When he smiled, his straight teeth showed white against his brown skin. "You can call me Lee."

I shook my head again, my gaze sliding unerringly to the fallen coffin. "Do you know who it is?"

"Not yet, Miss. Now, if you'll just go back out to the lobby..."

I nodded, letting tears flow freely down my face. He touched my arm, his hand warm and heavy against my skin, and gave me a gentle nudge toward the door. I took a step in that direction, then another one, and as soon as he turned away, I ducked behind the room divider folded against the back wall and dodged quickly toward the stage. I heard him shout as I neared the coffin but I ignored him, determined to see if it was...

I gasped as I came around another coffin and caught sight of the woman spilling from the topped casket onto the carpeted floor. My knees buckled and a sob emerged. I hit the ground, barely managing to soften the blow to my knees due to shock.

She looked frail draped over the coffin. Her hair shone under the overhead fluorescent lights. One slender arm reached in my direction, the fingernails torn and fingers painted with blood. More blood painted the front of her demure pink blouse, the ruffles at her throat weighed down by it.

Lipstick smeared across her face and her mouth was open in a silent scream. Wide gray eyes stared sightlessly toward me, already glazing in death.

Security stood behind me, two men whose bodies gave off an unnatural heat that barely touched the chill in my bones.

"Do you know her?" one of them asked.

I lifted a hand to my face and expanded my chest with air for the first time since I'd heard that scream. A tissue appeared in front of me. I took it, blowing my nose. Then I cleared my throat and finally spoke. "No. I thought it was someone else. But it isn't her."

Relief slipped through me, warming some of the chill that was making my teeth clack together. It finally sank in. It wasn't Pinella. "What happened?" I asked, not expecting them to answer me and surprised when they did.

"They panicked," the first guard said. "The crowd. When they realized she was dead, they all panicked and someone bumped the coffin." I looked up at him in time to see him grimace. "As if she needed more indignity thrust at her."

"May?" a familiar, shrill voice yelled.

The guard near the door tried and failed to contain the dual forces of nature barreling my way. "Ma'am, you can't go in there!"

As I had, Pinella ignored security, toddling toward me at

full speed on her leopard-skin heels with Shakespeare yipping angrily at the end of his leash. Since the little darling wasn't allowed in the diner, I'd left him in my room. How Pinella had gotten hold of him was beyond me. Shakes leaped into my arms, licking my face with a frantic kind of love. "Hey, buddy," I murmured into his sweet-smelling fur.

"Are you okay, dolly?" She stopped next to me and cupped my face in a cool, gnarled hand. "You're white as a sheet." She looked up at the two men, her expression filled with rage. "This girl is going into shock. What are you two galloops doing about it?"

They stuttered and twitched until she pointed an arthritic finger toward the coffee service on the table at the back of the room. "Hot tea. Now! And somebody needs to bring her a blanket."

As soon as they left, Pinella crouched down beside me. "I just wanted to get rid of them." She frowned. "But you do look too pale, dolly."

I gave her an impulsive hug, holding on tight. "I thought it was you. I thought you..." I couldn't say the words.

She returned my hug, patting me awkwardly on the back. "Oh, dolly. Did I forget to tell you I'm never going to die?"

I barked out a wet laugh. Mopping my face with the already drenched and tatty tissue, I sniffed. "I should have known that. How'd you get hold of Shakes?"

"I was heading to your room when the little guy dodged past the cleaning lady's cart and headed for the elevators. I grabbed him up and got his leash from your room, figuring you'd rather he was with me instead of annoying the cleaning crew." She winced. "You're going to want to leave a big tip for housekeeping. I only caught about half of the woman's rant, but I'm pretty sure he ate her feather duster and peed on the cart before he made his grand escape."

I sniffed, nodding. "That sounds like him."

"Now, stop your sniveling and tell me what we're dealing with. PoPo will be here soon and we need to know everything there is to know before they throw us out if we're going to catch the killer."

I stared at her a moment, my brain fighting to follow the segue she'd thrown me. Then it clicked. She was right. The police would surely make us leave, and I needed to see what I could see before then. Nodding, I climbed to my feet and stepped closer to the tumbled coffin and its grisly contents.

The woman looked to be around thirty years old. She was dressed in an elegant, dove gray suit with a pale pink silk blouse beneath the tailored jacket. Her silver-blonde hair was styled in a smooth, short bob, the strands framing a sharp jawline even in the disarray of death.

She lay on her side, her chest hidden beneath the outflung arm. "I can't see if she has a badge on."

"If she was wearing one before, the killer probably ripped it off," Pinella said in a surprisingly calm voice. "How was she killed?"

Staring at the half-moon of darkening blood at her throat, I swallowed hard. "Somebody cut her throat." I leaned down, getting a better look. "I also see some finger bruises."

Pinella nodded without flinching. "Jewelry? Tattoos?"

I stared at the older woman. "Who are you, and what have you done with Pinella?"

My neighbor chuckled. "I'm a woman of many facets," she said with a curve of her thin, painted lips. She nodded toward the woman on the floor. "Jewelry can tell us a lot about a person. Like the diamond studs in her ears."

She was right. The diamonds in the dead woman's earrings looked to be around two carats, nestled in an expensive platinum setting. Somebody loved her enough to spend thousands of dollars on a pair of earrings. I pulled out my phone and took several pictures. One small tattoo was visible beneath a white gold ankle bracelet. It was a single word in flowing script. "Love." I read aloud.

"We need to find the lover on the other end of that invisible tether," Pinella said, nodding.

The distant wail of sirens I'd been listening to for the last several minutes was suddenly much closer. Beyond the closed doors leading to the lobby, orders were suddenly being barked. By the time the double doors were flung wide, Pinella and I had moved to a spot several yards away from the body.

Unfortunately, the move didn't fool the man who was first through the door. He'd dealt with me before and didn't trust me any more than I trusted him.

Apparently my dog agreed with my low opinion of the man. Shakes growled low in his throat as Detective Robard strode in our direction.

3

S tanding about five-ten or eleven, the cop wasn't a big guy, but he had broad shoulders and his arms were thicker than my legs. Detective Robard was with the Asheville Police Department. We'd met before on another case, and I could honestly say that the only thing I liked about him was his 1973 Camaro. The low-slung sports car was silver with wide black racing stripes on the hood. It was a sweet ride.

"Why am I not surprised to find you in the middle of another murder," he asked me.

I waggled my fingers at him, trying to look harmless. "Hey, Detective. How's that Camaro?"

He blinked in surprise at my question. But to his credit, he recovered quickly. "My car is fine. You, however, are in big trouble. As usual." He reached into the pocket of his tatty tweed sports coat and came out with a pair of handcuffs.

I knew it was just bluster, but found myself wanting to make a run for it none-the-less. I frowned at the cuffs. "What are those for?"

"I understand you deliberately disrupted my crime scene after you were told to leave. Did you know the victim?"

"No," I admitted.

"What excuse could you possibly have for being in this room, messing up any potential evidence then?"

I hesitated, glancing toward Pinella. "I...thought I knew her."

Robard shook his head. "Uh, huh. "Do I have to cuff you or are you going to cooperate?"

Shakes yipped, his tail whipping high and fast as he sized up the detective's scuffed black loafers. I wasn't sure if the little guy was thinking about chewing the shoes or peeing on them, but I would heartily support either action at the moment.

Pinella started toward the cop, stumbling slightly as her heels caught on the rug. She batted fake lashes that looked like spider legs at him and pursed her wrinkled lips, her lipstick bleeding through the lines. "Well, hello, gorgeous," she said, "Who might you be?"

Robard reared back as if he'd been struck. "I'd be the detective in charge of this investigation. Who might you be, ma'am?"

She offered him her hand. "I'm Pinella Gerrard. I'm a coffin surfer in this here event." She dropped her lashes demurely, a ghastly picture of feigned innocence. "I'm so relieved you're here, officer. A big, strong man such as yourself."

Robard opened his mouth and then skimmed me a frown and clamped it shut again.

That was my cue. I stood up and walked over to Pinella. "Pinella is my neighbor and friend. She was very upset when she saw the body in the overturned coffin. I'm sure you can understand that."

Pinella nodded, folding in on herself and leaning heavily against me as if her kitten heels could barely hold her up. "I'm so grateful May was here when I needed her."

"Yip!" Shakes agreed, dancing on the end of his leash.

Robard's brown eyes narrowed on me. I could tell he wanted to call bull pucky on our act, but wasn't sure if it would backfire on him.

Pinella glanced up at me, her lips quivering. "Dolly, would you mind walking me to my room? I'm feeling a little woozy."

I pressed my lips together to keep from laughing. Pinella was a force of nature. I didn't think being hit by a charging water buffalo would even set her back on her heels. The buffalo would probably walk away with a black eye and a broken horn. "Of course. Come along. We'll get some hot tea into you."

Right on cue, Lee, the security guard approached with a paper cup. "I brought the tea," the big man said. For a man of his size, he'd approached more quietly than he should have been able to.

Pinella grabbed the cup and gave him a trembling smile. "Thank you, dearie. That's very kind."

"Dirk went to housekeeping for the blanket."

Robard's assessing gaze slid from us to the burly guard, his jaw tight.

"I'm going to take her upstairs," I told the confused security guard. "Thank you so much for the tea. That was very kind." I tugged on Pinella's arm and started for the door. "Walk fast," I said to her under my breath. "Robard smells a rat." Shakespeare was way ahead of us, happily bouncing toward the crowd in the lobby.

Pinella snorted out a laugh. "The only rat in this place is the killer. And you and me are gonna find him, dolly."

I nudged her with my shoulder. "You're a pretty good actress."

"Oh, I know."

"Did you have formal training."

"More practical than formal," she said, nodding enthusiastically. "I was married to a man I couldn't stand for ten years. He never guessed I wanted to poke his eyes out every time he opened his stupid mouth."

I'd barked out a laugh before I could stop myself.

Pinella winked at me.

"Ferth!" Robard called from behind us.

"Hurry," I urged Pinella, all but dragging her through the doors.

The crowd that had emptied into the lobby was mostly still there when we came out. On the heels of that thought, I realized the police had likely told them they couldn't leave. That was the moment it finally sank in.

The killer was probably in the hotel...trapped there with us. I swallowed hard.

"What is it, dolly?" Pinella asked. "You look like you've seen a ghost."

Scooping Shakes off the floor so he wouldn't get stepped on, I scanned the faces in the room, not sure what I was looking for. I saw a lot of worried expressions, some fearful ones, and a few that were angry.

People kept glancing at their phones as if they had somewhere else they needed to be.

It looked like there were more than a hundred people in the lobby, and I knew that, like me, not all of the convention-eers had attended the early morning session.

"MayBell?" Pinella's tone had turned worried. "What you thinkin' about, dolly?"

I forced my mind back to the reality of a murder that had way too many suspects. "I was just thinking I didn't envy the police trying to get to the bottom of this."

She made a face. "Good thing they have us to help them."

A man I didn't know pushed through the crowd, his face infused with angry color. I instinctively stepped in front of Pinella as he approached, his stride aggressive. "What happened in there? Did you see the body?"

Pinella tried to step around me but I wouldn't let her. "You'll need to talk to the police," I told him. "If you'll excuse us..."

He grabbed my arm when I tried to move away from him. "Hey!" I tried to shake him off. His grip tightened painfully. "Ouch, let go of my arm!" I spoke loudly, intentionally drawing the attention of the crowd. Immediately, other voices rose to meet mine.

"Let her go, man."

"Stop manhandling her, you bully!"

Likely sensing he wasn't on the right side of public opinion, he dropped my arm like a hot potato, lifting his hands in surrender. "Sorry. Emotions are high."

I eyed the man, wondering if I'd just met our killer. Ignoring the residual ache the man's grip had left behind, I linked arms with my neighbor and turned, melting into the crowd with Pinella tucked against my side.

"What do we do now?" Pinella asked as we finally emerged near the elevators.

Any hope of escaping to my room was dashed when I saw the uniforms standing in front of the elevators. I sighed.

"I guess we'll find a spot to sit and wait it out. They're going to want to talk to everyone here."

Pinella blanched. "Everyone?"

I nodded, feeling as miserable as she looked.

"That's going to take a while."

"It is." A familiar figure caught my eye in the crowd. The man was tall, over six feet, with broad shoulders and an unruly mop of dark hair. Thick, dark lashes framed stunning green eyes that scanned the room as if he were looking for someone. My PI's expression was grave, his gaze searching. "Eddie's here!" I told Pinella.

I'd never been so happy to see anyone in my life. I turned to my neighbor. "Sit over there on that bench, out of the way. I'm going to get him."

She nodded, unusually quiet. I suspected the situation was starting to sink in for her too. I dove into the crowd, keeping an eye out for the pushy guy as I made my way to Deitz. When I was within fifteen feet of him, I called his name, my voice getting lost in the rumble of conversation.

"...can't believe she's dead..."

"Someone took it. I hope I don't need any of those props or I'm going to be..."

"...bought red. I thought red shoes would look best..."

Eddie heard me the second time I called out, turning a relieved smile in my direction and changing course. I threw myself into his arms when he reached me. "I'm so glad you're here."

Shakes yipped his agreement, giving Deitz a wet kiss on the cheek.

Eddie held me tight, his heart pounding against my ear. "Me too. Tell me what happened."

"I will. But let's move. Pinella's waiting over there."

I took his hand and pulled him through the crowd after

me. The throng was slow to shift, the body language of most of the people tight and jerky as the reality of their predicament set in. More than one angry reaction scalded us as we fought though the undulating bodies.

We finally broke through the bulk of the crowd, emerging into a space near the elevators. I breathed in relief as cool air flowed over us. If the police didn't find some way to disburse the crowd, we were all going to melt from the excess body heat collecting in that lobby.

As we approached the bench, alarm set in. Pinella wasn't there.

"I thought you said Pinella was waiting," Eddie said, frowning.

"She was." I glanced down the hall to the restroom sign. "Maybe she ran into the ladies' room."

He nodded. "Tell me what happened while we wait for her."

I filled him in as succinctly as I could. He listened quietly, his gaze sliding over the crowd. When I'd finished, I realized he'd comprehended the same thing I had. His expression looked dire.

"This is bad, May," he finally said. "Soo many suspects. The police will lock down the hotel until they find the killer."

"Maybe they'll just get everybody's contact info and let us go," I said hopefully. I would be upset at missing out on my first convention, but I doubted the convention would continue anyway.

"Maybe." He didn't sound convinced.

I glanced toward the ladies' restroom. "Maybe I should go check on Pinella."

Eddie's gaze never stopped scanning the crowd. He looked even more worried than the situation warranted. I made a mental note to question him about that later. But first, I needed to find a wayward octogenarian rabble-rouser before she accidentally ran into a killer. "I'll be right back," I told Deitz, handing him Shakes.

He gave me a distracted nod and I took off down the hall. Some of the crowd had filtered into the hallways and I felt eyes on me as I hurried toward the women's restroom. I shrugged off the creeping sense of being watched and shoved the restroom door open. "Pinella?" Silence met my call. A beat later, a toilet flushed and a woman came out of the furthermost stall. She was about my height and strongly-built with pale skin and bright red hair. "Did you lose somebody?" she asked, her voice deep and slightly husky.

"I did, actually. An older woman dressed in..." I stuttered to a halt, unsure how to describe Pinella's clothing.

"Street corner chic with a dash of over the top?" The woman's lips curved in a wide smile.

I laughed. "That describes it perfectly. She was here?"

The woman nodded. "She passed me as I came in."

"How long ago was that?"

"Oh, maybe fifteen minutes." The woman blushed as if her statement indicted her in some way. "I hope you find her."

"Thanks," I said. "Have a great day."

Tugging her long sleeves over her hands in a nervous movement, she frowned. "That's not likely, I think." When I raised a brow in question, she clarified. "The murder?"

"Yes." I hesitated a beat and then decided to ask the question that had popped into my head. "How did you know?"

"That it was a murder?"

I nodded.

"I guess it could have been a suicide. But it's rare for a woman to commit suicide by slicing her own throat. In general, knives are too violent and messy for women. They mostly prefer poison."

"You saw the dead woman then? In the coffin?"

She nodded, her manner strangely calm. "Front and center. That shrill scream you heard...?" She raised a hand. "I'm appalled to admit that was me."

"I'm so sorry. That must have been horrible."

She shrugged. "It was."

"If you don't mind my saying, you seem to be taking it well."

She snorted. "If you'd been in here a few minutes ago, you wouldn't have thought so. I'm pretty sure I horked up everything I've eaten since last Sunday." She sighed. "I'm trying to put it into a more clinical framing. Taking a step back and dehumanizing the victim usually helps."

"It sounds like you have some experience with that."

"I have, actually. In my day job, I study and document the psychological profiles of killers and their victims."

"You work with the police?" I asked, intrigued.

"Occasionally. But mostly my books do the work for me." She smiled when I looked perplexed. "Law enforcement uses my research for training purposes."

"Wow, I'm impressed. How'd you land that gig?"

She shrugged. "It was pure luck, really. I documented the Dwight Crocker Maynard murders and someone at the training academy happened to read it. That got me in the door and I started taking requests for case studies after that."

"I remember the Maynard murders. They were terrifyingly fascinating."

She nodded. "He was a smart, creative killer. He studied

his victims for a long time, learning their interests, strengths and weaknesses, and then used the information against them."

"That time he drew that couple away from their campsite into the woods by creating a false blood trail," I said, shaking my head. "Pure genius."

"Yeah. He gambled that, given their love of cop and forensics shows they'd follow the trail themselves before calling the police. The gamble paid off." She grimaced. "For him anyway. It didn't work out so well for the victims."

I nodded my agreement. "What fascinating work." I found myself genuinely interested. "Are you here as a writer or a professional mourner?"

"Both, actually. I've done some PMing. It started as research but then I realized I enjoyed it. I'll write a book on the subject someday. But, for now, I'm enjoying the research."

A soft knock sounded on the door, followed by a deep, worried voice. "May? Is everything okay in there?"

Oh. Oops. I'd forgotten why I'd come into the bathroom. "I'll be right out," I called back. Smiling at the other woman, I said, "That's my boyfriend. It was nice chatting with you. Thanks for the information on Pinella."

She stared at me for a beat as if trying to figure out who I was talking about. Then her expression cleared. "Ah. Street corner chic with a dash of over the top."

I laughed, enjoying her sense of humor. "That's the one. Will you do me a favor? If you spot her, will you tell her May's looking for her?"

"Sure. Good luck finding her in that crowd. It's a madhouse out there."

∼

EDDIE WAS on his phone when I rejoined him. The noise in the hallway had tripled since I'd gone into the ladies' restroom and he was having trouble hearing whoever he was speaking to. He covered his ear and moved into a small alcove containing the water fountains. I watched the crowd as he finished up his conversation, seeing more worried expressions as reality sank in that we were basically prisoners until the cops let us go.

"I called Argh," Eddie told me when he returned. "He said APD had requested additional manpower for the witness interviews. He's on his way downtown now."

It didn't surprise me that my brother was coming downtown to pitch in. The Ashville police department and the Hillside PD where my dad and Argh worked sometimes shared manpower when it made sense. "What about Robard?"

Deitz shrugged. "I got the impression Argh was taking over for him."

Good. "Hopefully, Argh will clear me so I'll be free to move around."

Watching Eddie nod, I had a thought. "How did you get inside the hotel?" I asked. "The police had it locked down within minutes of the murder."

His gaze skittered away, colored with guilt.

My stomach clenched. "What did you do?"

"I didn't do anything. One of the cops was someone I knew."

The way his gaze wouldn't settle on mine, made the pain in my stomach double. "Let me guess. A woman you used to date?"

He shook his head, his sexy gaze sliding to finally lock on mine. "The sister of a PI I went through training with. We never dated."

"But you wanted to?"

"I didn't even consider it. Will would have been ticked off if I'd even looked at his baby sister that way."

"But you wanted to?" I repeated.

He expelled a frustrated breath. "I'm not a saint, May."

To both of our surprise, I laughed. "No, you aren't a saint. Far from it." When he bristled, I added. "And neither am I. I get jealous. It's ugly and I'm sorry. Can you forgive me?"

His expression softened and he pulled me into a hug. "I've given you reason to doubt my motives in the past. I understand. But if you could find a way past it, I'd be very grateful. When you look at me like that, with those beautiful, accusing blue eyes, I feel like I did when my gramma used to accuse me of stealing cookies off the baking sheet while they were still too hot to eat."

I grinned. "Did you? Steal the cookies?"

"Of course! I told you, I'm not a saint. I have a weakness for hot cookies and even hotter women." He winked.

I laughed.

Without warning, the wall next to us erupted in a spray of wood and shredded wallpaper.

4

The reality of a bullet slamming into the wall beside me was so stunning it took me a minute to react. I wasn't alone. The entire lobby stilled, the silence following the shot so fraught with confusion it would have been comical if it weren't so dire.

Eddie acted first. He shoved me into the alcove of a nearby office and screamed. "Down! Everybody down."

Another shot shattered the frosted door glass and screams tore the silence. Shakes yelped and dove at me, clawing at my legs to be picked up. I bent down to pick him up and a weight slammed into me. Shakes and I hit the carpet, Eddie sprawled over us. Panic had me fighting to get out from under him. Had he been hit?

"Eddie!" My scream was lost beneath a cacophony of noise as several more shots speared the lobby, sending people to the ground or racing for the door. I shoved against the floor, managing to partially dislodge my human anchor. "Eddie, are you shot?"

He grunted, grabbing my hands before I could roll him

off me with my movements. "I'm fine. Lay still. The police are here."

I stilled, realizing he was right. Uniforms flooded through the front doors and poured from the lecture room. My gaze caught on Argh and I screamed his name. He'd been scanning the crowd, his gun drawn. When he spotted us, he hurried over, his gaze still skimming the space for the shooter. He reached us and crouched down. "You've been hit," he told Eddie, as if the PI hadn't noticed the hole in his own flesh.

"I'm fine. It just grazed me. Did you guys get the shooter?"

My lungs filled with air as the weight lifted off my back. When I tried to get up, both Argh and Eddie pressed a hand against my back. "Stay down," they barked in unison. I groaned. "Great. Now I have two men bossing me around."

Shakes shivered under my arm, content to stay where he was.

Eddie's hand lay warm on my back. Argh shifted away and stood.

"Man down!" someone yelled from near the stairs. Sure enough, when the stairwell door opened to admit two uniformed cops, I glimpsed a man face-down on the landing. The door glass had been shattered and it appeared he'd been struck by an errant bullet. After a minute, the man started to move, even trying to get up before the uniformed officer stopped him from moving.

"Stay!" Argh barked as he turned and ran in that direction.

"Woof," I mumbled in irritation. Sitting up, I saw the blood on Eddie's shoulder. "We need to take care of that."

He nodded. "Ambulances will arrive soon. I'll make sure it gets bandaged."

"Will they let everyone leave now?" I asked, frowning at the chaotic scene around us. "People are sitting ducks in this lobby."

"That's likely what the shooter wanted," Eddie said. "But he won't get what he wants. They won't let the killer walk out of here hidden within the crowd."

I knew he was right, but that didn't make me any happier. "So, we're locked in with a killer. What could possibly go wrong?"

He reached out and squeezed my hand, wincing as the movement tightened the muscles around his wound. "If it makes you feel any better, the shooter clearly didn't try to hurt anybody. All the shots were high. Except for a few ricochets, nobody was injured."

"Are you all right, dolly?"

My head snapped up and I saw Pinella hurrying toward me. Relief razored through me. "Pinella! Where have you been? I was worried about you."

The octogenarian stopped next to me and lowered herself awkwardly to the nearby bench. Eddie leaped up and helped when her knees seemed to lock up midway through the action. "Thanks, handsome," Pinella said with a saucy wink.

"Sorry to worry you, dolly. I just wanted to go up to my room and change my shoes. Those heels were killing me."

She nodded toward her long, narrow feet, which were currently ensconced in a pair of shoes with the same type of kitten heels on them.

"Are those better?" I asked doubtfully.

"So much better," she said on a sigh. "What happened here? Why is that woman over there wailing and bleeding?" Her gaze shot to Eddie's shoulder. "And what happened to the stud?"

Eddie winced at the dehumanizing language, shaking his head.

Pinella didn't notice. "I leave you alone for five minutes and look what happens," she lamented.

I bit my tongue. She'd left me alone for far more than five minutes. But I set that aside for the obvious question. "How'd you get upstairs? The police have been guarding all the exits."

Her lips curved, her messy lipstick creating a garish caricature of a smile. "Ned told me there was a back stairwell leading from the kitchen. Only the kitchen staff uses that stairwell. PoPo probably doesn't know about it."

"Who's Ned?" Eddie asked.

"The bartender. He was so kind and helpful."

"Bartender?" I really didn't like the strident quality of my question. Her antics should have ceased to surprise me long ago. "You've been in the bar too?"

"Of course, dolly." She gave us a poor excuse for a shudder, clearly faked. "I needed a nip to warm the chill from my bones. So much trauma for a middle-aged but still very attractive woman."

Eddie turned his head and I knew he was hiding a smile. I stared at her, my lips flapping unattractively. There was so much wrong in that statement, I wasn't sure where to start. "It's nine-thirty in the morning."

She nodded. "I'm pretty sure it's after five in the UK."

I stared at her. "Maybe, but you're not in the UK. You're here. Where it's nine-thirty AM."

She laughed. "Pull that giant stick out of your as..."

"Pinella," Eddie said with a suspicious wobble in his voice. "Did you see any police on the back stairs?"

Slamming my lips closed, I realized I'd been focusing on the wrong thing. Eddie was right, if the stairs from the kitchen were unmanned, the shooter could have escaped that way after the shooting. I glanced at the restaurant doors across the lobby. They were closed and the place looked dark. But that didn't mean someone couldn't have cracked the doors open and taken potshots at the unsuspecting crowd.

Pinella shook her head. "No uniforms on that stairway. But I saw one detective slipping into the stairwell as I was grabbing my snack."

Grabbing a snack? I dropped my head into my hands. "Jeezopete," I murmured.

"How did you know he was a detective?" Eddie asked. His gaze had sharpened, his expression going hard.

My neighbor looked offended. "Please. You don't think I can recognize a PoPo when I see one? I can spot a cop from a mile away."

"Humor me," Eddie said.

"This one was small but meaty. He was wearing a dark suit and had a gun. His eyes were cold and his hair was really short. If he wasn't a detective, he was a Fibber."

"Fibber?" I asked.

"FBI. Lands, dolly. Don't you watch TV?" Her eyes sparkled. "He was one pair of dark glasses away from Men in Black. Maybe we have space aliens in the hotel."

I was pretty sure we did. And their leader wore kitten heels. "Did you see where he went?"

"Nah. I was focusing on my Caesar salad with chicken by then."

My mouth fell open. "You made an entire meal before coming back out here?"

"It wasn't any great trick. The salad was already made up. All I needed to do was add some of that cold lemon-pepper chicken from the fridge and toss it with dressing."

My stomach growled at the thought. I was on the verge of asking if she thought she could make me a salad when Argh arrived to poo on my potential party.

"What are you three up to?"

We looked at him with an array of expressions. Eddie's was amused. Mine was annoyed. Pinella's was R-rated, bordering on X.

"Hey, gorgeous," she said, sidling up to him and winking her long, spindly lashes in her favorite "come hither" display. "Why don't you and I go sit someplace private and I'll give you a sit-rep."

Argh frowned, then skimmed me a look. "I blame you for this."

"Ah!" I objected. "Jump back, superpatch. Pinella's her own woman. I have zero control over her."

My neighbor's chuckle was deep and flirty. "Truth. I'm my own..." she tried to press her boobs into his arm. They landed somewhere down around his hip. "*Woman.*"

Argh jumped like he'd been shot. I had a sneaking suspicion he would have preferred a bullet. "Anyway," he said, returning his deepening glare to me. "Tell me about this shooter."

"I don't know anything about him," I said. "Why do you assume I know something?"

Pinella opened her mouth and I shifted my weight in her direction, surreptitiously pressing my shoe lightly over her toes in warning.

"I'm pretty sure the shots came from over there, near the restaurant," Deitz told my brother.

Argh followed his line of sight. "Yeah, the trajectory of the bullets supports that."

Eddie nodded. "Those slugs in the wall look like nine mils."

Argh nodded. "I'll have a uniform cut the bullets out." His glare found me again. "Don't touch them."

I gasped in outrage. "How did I turn into the bad guy here?"

"Because when there's trouble you're always in the middle of it," Argh growled.

I glanced at Eddie for support. He shrugged, clearly agreeing with my brother.

Jerks.

"She's not *always* in the middle," Pinella said. "She was eating breakfast in the diner over there when that woman was gacked."

"Gacked?" Argh asked, again glancing at me.

That one he *could* blame me for. "Iced, liquidated, floated with da fishes, paired with the grim reaper in the great dance of death, ripped from this mortal coil. Should I go on?"

"MayHilarious," Argh growled, his eyes sparkling with reluctant humor. "I oughta,"

I nodded. "Yes. You probably oughta. But you won't. So, can we move on? What did you learn about our victim?"

He laughed, but the humor was gone. "Nice try MayNot. Stay out of this."

"Or what?" I asked, my stubborn coming up in a big way.

"Or I'll tell the Lieutenant."

Shakes barked, his soft fan of a tail beating the air high and fast behind him. He clearly wasn't happy my brother was going to tattle on me to our dad. Scooping up my little hero, I tapped my palm against his tiny paw and said, "Solidarity." He kissed me on the nose.

Argh rolled his eyes. "I don't care what the rodent says, you are not to put yourself into the path of this killer, MayBell Ferth. Are we clear?"

Shakes growled softly and then sneezed as Argh glared at him.

"Whatever," I said.

"May..."

Ignoring his warning tone, I turned on my heel and headed across the lobby. I waited near a grouping of eight-foot-tall bamboo palms for my partners in crime to catch up. While I waited, I eyed the restaurant doors. Did I dare go inside? If the shooter had fired from there, he might have left something behind. I didn't want to disrupt the crime scene and possibly allow him to get away. But the police didn't seem too interested in the possibility that the shooter fired from that spot.

I glanced back and saw Pinella, her arm looped in Eddie's as they strolled my way. Feeling my face fold into a thoughtful frown, I smoothed out my brow. The last thing I wanted was worry wrinkles at the ripe old age of thirty-umph.

Catching my neighbor's eye, I motioned for her to hurry. She gave Eddie a tug and he turned to look a question at her. He'd been talking to someone. In the swirling crowd, I couldn't see who it was. He raised a finger when he saw me looking and released Pinella, turning back to the person I couldn't see.

Pinella swayed toward me, tottering only slightly on her slender heels. "That man of yours is better at gettin' information than you, dolly. You should take lessons."

"What do you mean?"

The crowd split apart as two EMTs pushed through with their gurneys of wounded and headed toward the front doors. That was when I saw Eddie's companion's face.

And my blood flash-fired.

He was speaking to a uniformed cop named Sarah. I'd

seen her before, at another crime scene. Officer Sarah was a beauty, with smoldering blue eyes, perfect burgundy lips, and a tidy and curvaceous figure. She even looked good in the shapeless uniform.

I bit back a surge of jealousy, trying to give Eddie the benefit of the doubt. He'd never given me any reason to think he was seeing other women. It was just that women loved my PI, and he was always friendly to them, which, Pinella was right, generally helped us get more information than we otherwise would have.

I sighed.

"You know he's just pumpin' her for information, right?" my elderly neighbor nudged. "That boy's crazy about you."

I knew he was. And I knew he wasn't flirting with the beautiful Sarah. Still... "You're right. Women respond to him. He uses that to his advantage. But he's always kind and never leads them on." Some of the heat left my face and I took a deep breath. I was an idiot.

"You could do the same thing, you know. I've seen how these alpha males look at you."

I winced. "I'm not good at flirting."

Pinella eyed the gorgeous Eddie as he strode back our way. "You got to be doin' somethin' right, dolly."

"What did you learn?" I asked as he approached.

He wrapped a warm hand around my arm, gently tugging me toward the diner. "Come on. Let's get away from all these cops."

The hotel had two restaurants off the lobby. One was a fancy dining establishment which offered only lunch and dinner. Brisard's was its name. A more unimaginatively named, The Diner, was geared toward more casual dining. It was the diner we headed toward, eschewing the fancier place, which wasn't open. If the shooter had used one of the restaurants for cover, it would have been Brisard's, because there would be no witnesses.

A waitress hurried over as we entered The Diner. She smiled at Shakes, apparently not worried about the no-dog rule, and scratched him under the chin. Giving us an apologetic smile, she said, "With everything that's going on, the grill is closed, folks. But I can get you something to drink. It's on the house."

"We'll take three iced teas, please," I said.

"Sure, hon. Sit wherever you like."

Eddie tugged my hand toward the back of the restaurant. He motioned for Pinella to slide in across from us and then lowered himself onto the bench beside me.

"What's going on?" I asked him. "What did Sarah tell you?"

Eddie lowered his head toward mine, his soft voice bathing my ear with warm air. "The dead woman tried to change rooms yesterday because someone was harassing her. She didn't give the hotel any names, but the manager told Sarah the woman had seemed really freaked out."

I thought of the scene by the elevator the night before. Could the dead woman have been the female voice I'd heard? "There's something I need to..."

Eddie held up a finger and leaned away from me as the waitress arrived.

"Can I have some sugar for my tea, dearie?" Pinella asked the young woman.

"It's right there in that container..." The waitress's voice trailed off as she eyed the empty sweetener dish. "That's weird. I could have sworn that was full a minute ago." Shaking her dark head, she gave us a tense smile. "I'll get you a refill."

I narrowed my eyes on Pinella until she bristled.

"What? They're probably charging us for that sugar anyway. I might as well get some use out of it."

"The drinks are on the house, Pinella," I reminded her.

She simply shrugged, patting the sugar bulge in her purse.

"The victim was in room 512," Eddie told me.

My eyes went wide. "Sarah gave you a room number? Can't she get in trouble for that?"

He shook his head. "It was written down on her clipboard. She forgot to hide it when I stopped her." He grinned wickedly and, in that moment, I would have forgiven him anything.

"Great. Now we just need to figure out how to get up to Room 512 to check it out."

"We might..." Pinella stopped and beamed at the waitress who'd just returned.

"Here you are, ma'am. I'm really sorry about that."

"No worries. Thank you so much, dearie."

The woman had barely turned back around before Pinella was upending the contents of the dish into her purse.

I gasped. She winked.

"Did you even add any sugar to your tea after all that?"

She grimaced. "Ugh. Why would I do that?"

"There's a reason we're in this diner," Eddie said, somehow staying on track despite our banter. "Have you noticed the two restaurants share a wall?"

I thought about it and he was right. They were located on the same side of the lobby. "You think they're connected?"

"Probably not. But I'll bet they both feed into the same back stairwell."

Pinella indicated a burly young man with bushy brown hair who was wearing a soiled white apron. "Then what are we waiting for?" she asked. "Let's go. The cooks and waitstaff are all out here. The kitchen is empty."

"Everybody out!" a sharp male voice called into the diner. "Nobody should be in this restaurant." He glared at the employees. "Weren't you informed of that?"

The woman who'd served us shook her head, a mulish expression overtaking her face. "Nobody's told us anything except that we couldn't sell food. If you all would get your heads out of your a..."

"We'll leave," a big, dark-skinned man said, throwing a significant glance toward the waitress. "We just need a minute to get our things from the back."

The uniformed officer's glare deepened. "Make it quick." He glanced across the room and fixed Pinella with a look. "You too, ma'am. Come on out of here."

Eddie and I had ducked low in the booth, our heads not visible above the high wooden back from where the cop stood.

Pinella gave the nasty cop her best, flirtatious smile. "Of course, officer." She clicked her nails on the table in front of us. "You two owe me one," she said, murmuring softly. "I'll keep him distracted."

A moment later, Pinella was all but climbing the alarmed young man, her spider-leg lashes beating against her over-rouged cheeks as she hunted him like a jungle cat chasing a wounded zebra.

Footsteps sounded nearby and the waitress jerked to a stop beside the booth, her eyes going wide.

Eddie put a finger over his lips. I silently begged her not to give us away.

Her lips curved in a slight smile as the cop yelled at her again.

"Hurry up, sweetheart. What are you doing over there?"

"Oh no, he din't!" I said softly enough that only she and Deitz could hear. Deitz shook his head.

The waitress raised her brows to tell me that, yes, he had. She surreptitiously slid her order pad onto the table with one hand and grabbed it with the other. "Untwist your panties, YMCA. I'm just getting the pad I left over here."

She turned away and headed for the door, calling to her companions as she left. Two minutes later, the restaurant was empty and quiet. Eddie and I stayed put for another couple of minutes before we slid from the booth and headed for the kitchen.

"What if there's no staircase back there?" I asked.

"Then we'll find another way upstairs. There has to be a way up to the other floors from the restaurants."

The kitchen was smaller than I'd expected. The counters were covered in food and debris and the room was permeated with the scent of hot oil. A bucket filled with soapy water sat near the door, a wet spot around the bucket testifying to the fact that someone had been cleaning up when the attack happened in the hotel.

A burger congealed on a stainless-steel countertop, cold

fries piled next to it on the white ceramic plate. Someone had probably been in the process of decorating the plate with lettuce, tomato and pickles when the shots were fired. Condiments trailed over the counter and dripped onto the floor.

I scooped Shakes up to keep him from eating everything he found on the floor.

Eddie and I started opening doors, discovering a walk-in refrigerator, a closet stuffed with cleaning supplies, an over-sized freezer, a supply room, and finally, a door leading to a stairwell. We hurried through the door and jogged up the stairs to the fifth floor. Opening the stairwell door a crack to peer out into the hall, we realized our fatal mistake.

The police had a guard on the door to room 512.

Of course they would.

Eddie and I shared a look and then ducked back, easing the door closed.

"Now what?" I asked.

"Now we wait for an opening," he said, nodding toward the landing floor. "You might as well make yourself comfortable. This could be a long wait."

I sighed and did as he suggested, settling myself into the corner and folding my hands in front of me to keep them off the floor. I tried not to think about what I was sitting on and leaning against. Eddie stood to one side of the small, narrow window in the stairwell door, his gaze locked on the over-weight, gray-haired cop standing in front of 512. The cop looked bored and unhappy to be there.

I didn't feel like chatting, and was worried the sound would carry anyway, so I closed my eyes and rested against the wall, the stress of the last couple of days finally getting the best of me. I woke up some time later, unsure how long it had been since I'd drifted off. It took me only a minute to realize Eddie and Shakes were no longer in the stairwell with me. I shoved to my feet and groaned as all my muscles contracted unhappily. I was getting too old for sleeping upright on a hard floor. Come to think of it, pretty much everybody would be too old for that.

A quick peek down the hallway told me the middle-aged cop was gone. He'd probably gone to the restroom in the lobby or to grab a cup of coffee.

Had Eddie gone into 512 without me?

I opened the door just wide enough to slip through, and hurried down the hall. Stopping outside the victim's door, I leaned close and listened, hearing nothing.

Where had Eddie and Shakes gone?

I pulled my sleeve over my hand and tried the knob.

Locked. No surprise there.

Glancing up and down the hall, I spotted an abandoned housekeeping cart. There was probably little to no chance there'd be a master key on that cart. But I had no options, so I decided to give it a try. At the same time, invisible fingers of worry gripped my lungs, making it hard to breathe. I was all too aware that the police would likely be back any minute, and I couldn't afford to get caught snooping.

There was no key on the cart. There were only a lot of towels, both clean and dirty, as well as other things like TP and tissues, small complimentary bottles of toiletries, and coffee refills. I slumped against the wall, my mind blanking on what to do next.

Then I heard voices. Harsh whispers, actually. Panic sheared through me. Looking around, I saw no place to conceal myself. I might be able to hide behind the ice maker at the end of the hall, but I'd never make it there in time. So, I did the only thing I could do. I yanked dirty towels out of the laundry bag and climbed inside, pulling the laundry over my head as the voices grew near.

The whispers stopped nearby. My heart pounded in my ears and I was sure the people could hear it.

"...gonna think I killed her," the first voice growled.

"You don't know..." the second voice said in a harsh whisper.

"I do know. And so do you. I need to go to the police. Talk to them."

"Don't you dare!" the other voice hissed.

A stairwell door slammed shut in the distance. The conversation stopped and I closed my eyes, praying the two speakers didn't decide it would be a good idea to hide in the dirty laundry bin.

"We need to get out of here," the first voice said.

"If you tell them anything, I'll make sure you regret it."

Someone was threatening murder? Could it be our killer? My thoughts roiled and spun. I needed to get a look at the speakers. One of them might have killed that woman.

"What about the other guy?"

I blinked, my focus returning to their conversation. *Other guy? Did they mean Deitz?*

"I'll take care of him. Just keep your mouth shut."

Another door slammed in the stairwell above, closer than the last. Were the police searching the floors?

Silence fell and I assumed the whisperers had left. I waited a minute and then realized I needed to get out of there before the police arrived on the fifth floor. Shoving towels out of my way, I started to stand. But didn't get far.

A fist came out of nowhere, heading for my face. I flinched away, turning my head in time to avoid knuckles to the nose, but got a fist to the forehead instead.

That had to hurt the man who'd delivered the punch as much as it hurt me. But I doubted he was as woozy as I was.

"Get the door!" a husky voice yelled as the cart jerked and I fell back into the bin. Damp towels engulfed me, their sour scent filling my nostrils. Then the intention behind the barked order sank in and I tried to rise. But the person pushing the cart gave it a final shove and it sailed through the door, hit the edge of the stairs and fell over, plunging downward in a series of teeth-chipping drops. At the bottom the cart tipped all the way over and dumped me out onto the concrete landing. I managed to keep from landing on my face, but just barely. My bones jarred from the impact and pain ratcheted through every bone and joint in my body.

Another door slammed shut above me and footsteps pounded downward. "May?"

I looked up at Eddie and blinked, seeing duplicates. "Two Eddies?" I muttered, clenching my aching head. "I'll never survive the stress."

Beside the double Deitz, was a double Shakes to keep him company. "Hey, buddy. Where'd you go?"

Eddie gently helped me into a sitting position, his expression filled with worry. "He was making a lot of noise when I tried to leave him behind, so I took him with me." Deitz gave me a quick once over. "What hurts?"

"Everything."

He looked up to the riser above, frowning. "How'd you fall down the stairs with a laundry cart?"

"I wasn't with it so much as inside it. And I didn't fall. I was pushed."

"Must have been my two friends." He rubbed his cheek and I noticed it was red and swollen.

"They hit you too?"

"Caught me stepping out of the fifth-floor landing. When that cop left, I thought I'd try to break into the room before he came back. They struck before I even knew they were there."

"Did you recognize the man who hit you?"

He shook his head. "I didn't even see him."

"How do you know there were two of them if you didn't see them?"

"I was still slightly aware as they hauled me upstairs and into a room that was under construction. I must have passed out and woke up to my wrists and ankles taped together. Fortunately, the idiots used painter's tape. It broke easily."

"What about Shakes?" I asked, pulling the little guy closer.

Eddie shrugged. "He was in the hallway when I left the room. I think he might have bitten the guy who was carrying him and gotten away. They must have just decided to leave him."

"What floor were you on?"

"The tenth, I think. I've been working my way down while trying to avoid the police. We need to get moving. The guards are changing on some of the floors."

That explained the slamming doors.

I held up my hand and Eddie took it, pulling me gently to my feet. "Come on. Let's go search the victim's room. We're not going to get another chance."

Eddie made quick work of the lock on the hotel room door. Though I was happy he was able to get us inside, the ease with which he breached it made me distinctly uncomfortable. "I'm never staying in a hotel ever again," I told him.

He waggled his brows. "Or, you could just bring me along for protection."

I barked out a laugh and agony speared my brain. "Ah!" I

rubbed the spot on my head where the guy had punched me.

"You're going to have a nice knot there," Eddie said. "It's already turning purple."

I tugged my hair over the spot. "You should see the other guy."

His expression darkened, his eyes going cold. "I fully intend to."

Deitz ushered Shakes and me into the room ahead of him, looking both ways down the hall before ducking inside with us. Wasting no time beginning my search, I pulled the closet door open and shoved clothing aside to search the floor. Then I spent a few minutes going through the pockets of the victim's clothing.

"Do you need gloves?" Eddie asked. "We don't want to leave prints behind."

I held up my sleeve-covered hands. "Mine are built in."

Slapping on his own acrylic gloves, he started searching. A beat later, I heard drawers opening and closing. Shakes trotted into the closet when I opened the door, snuffling around the clothes as I searched for anything that might lead to our killer.

He seemed particularly interested in a pair of khaki slacks, rising up on his back legs to sniff the pockets. "What did you find, buddy?" I shoved a hand into the pockets of the trousers, nearly missing a tiny piece of paper in the last one. I tugged it out and looked at what appeared to be the corner of a well-worn piece of paper. In addition to a small red stain that looked like catsup... probably what had inter-ested my always-foraging canine sleuth...the slip of paper held a series of numbers. "I found something. Or Shakes did."

Deitz was standing near the dresser that held the television set, staring at two plastic glasses and a bottle of wine. One glass had the dregs of wine on the bottom. One appeared to hold only water. The glass with wine dregs was also stained at the lip with lipstick. His head came up and he looked at me as I approached. I handed him the piece of paper. "It's a number. I found this in a pocket."

The note read 8305260914. "What do you think it means?"

"No idea. It could be a phone number." He pulled out his phone and dialed. The line rang several times before a message came on. The voice was heavily accented. Taking a chance, Eddie left a message. "Hello. My name is Eddie Deitz. I'm a private investigator in the Asheville, North Carolina area. I have some questions for you about a local murder. Can you return this call at..." He rattled off his phone number and disconnected.

Seeing me staring at him, he shrugged. "It's worth a try."

I nodded. It was. "Hopefully you didn't just call the killer."

He pulled me close, gently kissing my purple forehead. "As long as I stay out of stairwells and laundry carts I should be okay."

"Har," I told him, a grin teasing my lips. "Are we done here?"

"I need to search the bathroom."

We found nothing more incriminating than the fact that our victim had filled her makeup bag with the complimentary toiletries. The dead woman and Pinella would get along great.

We escaped the room and were nearly to the stairwell when the elevator dinged in warning. We barely made it inside the stairwell before a different, younger uniformed police officer stepped out of it. We hurried back down to the first floor and stopped, eyeing a second door leading to the stairs. "I'll bet a week's pay that leads to Brisard's."

I wasn't taking that bet.

"We need to see if there's anything the police missed," Eddie said.

"What if they're still inside?" I asked, knowing by the way Deitz was easing toward the door, that he'd already made up his mind. He was going in.

"We'll be careful. I doubt they gave the place more than a cursory look. The shooter would be stupid to hang out there. He probably came, fired off a few shots to keep everybody off balance, and then left again."

"But why? What would he gain by that?"

"I don't know yet. It's possible the shots weren't completely random. Maybe he suspects somebody saw him kill that woman." He frowned and I wondered if he was thinking...like I was...that a lot of those shots navigated toward us.

"Okay," I said. "Let's give it a look. The sooner we figure out who our killer is, the sooner we can dump what we find into Argh's lap and I can get back to my convention."

"Woof!" agreed Shakes.

6

The casing was wedged between the wall and a stack of high chairs next to the podium. Shakes was snorfling around the high chairs, no doubt smelling all sorts of spilled goodies on their scarred wooden surfaces. "I've got something," I called out to Deitz, drawing him across the restaurant to the spot where I crouched near the doors. "It looks like a bullet casing." I reached toward the metal object but stopped when Deitz called out to me. "Don't touch it!"

He crouched next to me and shone a small penlight into the space. "Nine mil."

I knew enough about firearms to know nine-millimeter handguns were popular with the police. "He must have picked up the rest," I told Eddie.

Eddie took a picture of the casing in place, and then took more shots around it to show the location. "The fact that the shooter policed his brass tells me he isn't just some yahoo with a gun. He knows what he's doing."

I nodded in agreement. "Are you going to share the location of that casing with Argh?"

"Only Argh," he said, giving me a look that said he was thinking the same thing I'd been thinking. The shooter might have been a cop.

I sighed. "I guess I'm going to have my ears chewed off again by Superpatch."

Deitz threw an arm around my shoulders and hauled me in for a kiss on my cheek. "I'm not worried about you. I know you can take him."

The lobby was quiet and empty when we emerged from the diner a few minutes later. Two uniformed officers guarded the front doors. The male cop wasn't paying any attention to the lobby or us because he was too busy flirting with the lovely Officer Sarah.

Sarah straightened away from the wall when she spotted us leaving the diner. She put a hand on her gun and stopped, seeming to recognize Eddie. She frowned.

He threw up his hands as if in surrender and laughed silently before turning away and dropping a hand to the small of my back. "Just keep walking unless they call out to us."

He didn't have to tell me twice. We made it nearly to the elevator before Sarah called Deitz' name.

"Let me do the talking," he mumbled softly. Turning around, he gave Sarah his best ligament-melting smile. "Hey, Officer. Did you guys let everybody go to their rooms?"

Sarah seemed torn between the smile and the question. Her gaze flicked to me and she frowned slightly. "What were you two doing in the diner?"

I opened my mouth to confess everything. Fortunately, Deitz knew me well. He moved slightly to block me from Sarah's view. "I know we were supposed to evacuate, but I was starving. I talked May into staying and eating a burger and fries with me."

Shakes barked, his button eyes sparkling with interest.

"Shakes got a burger too," I said, grinning.

Sarah's frown deepened. "They weren't supposed to serve food after the attack."

"Oh," he said, shaking his head. "They didn't. Don't tell on me. I kind of helped myself to the fixins'."

She stared at him for a minute and then nodded. "Tell you the truth, I gave some thought to getting a snack myself. I haven't eaten since breakfast."

"I get hangry when I don't eat," I told her, smiling.

She ignored my attempt to be friendly and refocused her attention on my boyfriend. "Everybody was cleared to go to their rooms a few minutes ago. There are officers on every floor, at the elevators and the stairs. Once you go into your room, you'll need to stay there except for carefully controlled events."

Eddie nodded as if he was perfectly okay with that. "No problem. Thanks for the information." He waved. "I'll talk to you later."

"We can't go to our rooms," I told him as we stepped onto the elevator.

He smiled one last time at Sarah and waved. The doors eased closed. "What floor are you on?" he asked me.

"Five."

"Five it is."

"But, the killer won't stay in his room. How are we going to catch him if we're locked in?"

"We aren't. Unless I miss my guess, he'll catch *us*. We just need to be ready for it."

"Explain."

"No time right now. When the elevator stops, you need to leave the car fast and distract the cop stationed there."

"What are you going to do?"

"I'm going to duck into the ice room. Assuming the argument you heard was relevant, the killer may have had a room on your floor. Which is handy for us because he'll want to get out of the hotel. I'm guessing he'll try to make a break for the stairs. If he can get to the parking lot level, he might be able to find a way out of the building. If he tries that, I'm going to be right behind him."

The elevator stopped and dinged out a warning that the doors were about to open. I looked at Eddie. "Be careful. This guy is dangerous."

He nodded, pulling me into a quick hug before ducking into the corner as the door opened.

Shakes jumped up and put his tiny paws on Eddie's shins, earning himself a scratch behind the ears. "Take good care of her, buddy."

The cop wasn't standing in front of the elevator as I'd expected. I pulled in a deep breath and dove deep into my acting portfolio. By the time I rounded the corner and stepped into the hallway, tears were already glistening in my eyes.

The uniformed officer looked up from the spot where he'd been standing. Unless I missed my guess, he'd been eyeing the dregs of a room service tray as if considering taking a bite out of the discarded pastry there. He blinked at me, surprise at being caught ogling the cheese Danish clear on his plain face. "What are you doing out here?" he asked. "You're supposed to be in your room." Playing his part, Shakes gave the man a single, interested bark, wagging his tail.

I hurried past him, drawing his attention away from the elevator lobby. I gasped out a sob, placing a shaking hand over my face. "I can't believe I'm here. This is just my luck to get caught up in this kind of mess." I covered my face with both hands and let loose, the sobs loud enough to cover any small sounds Deitz would make behind us.

The officer moved closer, lifting a hand and then looking at it as if he didn't know what to do with it. "Miss...are you going to be all right?"

I let my knees buckle, one of my better "overcome by grief" moves. He leaped for me, grabbing me under the arms and lowering me gently toward the ground. "She was my friend," I wailed. "She was just so vital and alive, you know?"

The cop nodded, patting my shoulder with obvious unease. He *didn't* know. But he was going to commiserate if it killed him. "Your friend is dead?"

I wailed louder and he twitched, patting faster. "I'm sorry. That was insensitive, wasn't it? My sister always tells me I'm stupid around women."

I covered my face to hide a smile. That sounded exactly like something a sister would say. I sniffled loudly and reached up to cover his hand on my shoulder. "You're not stupid at all." I gave him a watery smile, scraping a hand beneath my wet eyes. "You're right." She's...g...g...gone." I hiccupped a sob. "And I'll never see her again." I could feel Deitz's gaze on me but didn't dare look. He'd be laughing. Or maybe frowning, given that he'd been snared by the same mourning song the first time we'd met.

Actually, that wasn't entirely true. At the time, he hadn't believed a single watery sniff. But I'd given him the show of his life nevertheless.

"Here," the cop said, his dark brown eyes downcast as he handed me a slightly mangled tissue. "It's clean."

I nodded, using it to dry my tears. "You're very kind."

"You knew the victim?"

I nodded.

"Maybe you could tell me about her?"

I frowned.

"Anything you can tell me might help us find her killer."

I blinked, widening my tear-drenched gaze in his direction. "Killer?"

"Yes. You knew she'd been murdered, right?"

I gasped, a hand over my mouth. "No! Oh no. That just makes it worse!" I wailed.

Shakes whined and licked my arm.

The officer looked perplexed. "I'm sorry. I thought you knew."

Shaking my head, I said, "Nobody could kill her. Everybody loved her." I smiled sadly. "You didn't know her, but I'll bet you'd have loved her." Shakes wagged his tail, his gaze locked onto the door leading to the ice maker. I scooped him up, praying he didn't alert the cop to Eddie's presence. Burying my face in his fur, I gave a shaky sob. "Everybody loved Snowball."

There was a taut silence. I kept my face buried in Shakes' fur, both to keep him from whining for Eddie, and because I was afraid I'd start laughing if I looked at the cop's face.

"Snowball is your…?"

"Cat," I said, huffing out a sob. "My sweet little furball. My neighbor just called to tell me she'd passed."

"Oh."

I pressed my face harder into my dog's soft fur, shoulders shaking as I imagined his face.

"Okay. Well, let's get you into your room."

When I threw him an appalled look, he added. "So, you can grieve in private."

"Right. I should grieve privately. I'm being too loud, aren't I. I'm so sorry." I pushed to my feet and gave Shakes' leash a little tug. "Come on, buddy. Let's go do a memorial wall for Snowball."

Shakes made an unhappy sound, then sneezed before falling into step beside me.

"I hope you're feeling better soon," the cop called out. "Maybe we could have a drink later."

I swung around, giving him a shocked glance.

"I mean. You know. To toast poor Snowball."

If the cop heard the suspicious cough down the hallway behind him, he gave no indication of it. "I'd love to toast my sweet furball."

He grinned.

A handsome face popped around the doorway at the end of the hall. Deitz glared my way.

My lips twitched. "Maybe I'll see you later, Officer..."

"Loveless," the cop said. "Todd Loveless."

I barely covered my mouth and coughed in time to ward off the laugh.

7

The woman on the other end of the line didn't waste any time. She got right to the point. "This is a courtesy call to let you know the scheduled eleven AM lecture will be held as planned."

"Are you sure?" I glanced at the clock next to the bed. It was ten-fifty.

"Yes, ma'am. The organizer asked us to call all of the attendees."

And her tone told me she was feeling the pressure.

"Okay. Thanks for letting me kn..." The line went dead. Shaking my head, I hung up. I stared at the door and chewed my bottom lip. What if Eddie needed me and I was downstairs? I thought about calling him, then realized I couldn't risk anyone hearing his phone ring. Even a ding announcing a text could be bad news if Loveless was nearby.

The irony of my being flirted with by a guy named Loveless made me grin.

I mentally kicked myself. *Focus, May!*

I had a cheering thought. Maybe Loveless would be patrolling the other end of the hallway when I left my room.

Maybe he'd be scarfing somebody's leftover cheeseburger or something and I'd get a chance to speak quickly to Deitz.

Besides, the lecture was the perfect place to learn more about our victim.

Feeling better, I quickly changed my clothes, brushed my teeth, and clipped a leash on my partner in crime. "Come on, little man. We have some sleuthing to do and a lecture to pretend to listen to."

Shakes yipped happily and ran to the door, his steps a bit prancier than usual. He was ready to charm a few potential witnesses. Nobody knew how to soften up a mark better than the Pomeranian Devil.

We stepped into the hall and I was happy to see that Officer Loveless was talking to another young woman at the far end of the hall. If he truly was loveless, it wasn't for lack of trying. The cop barely gave me a glance when I waved and turned with a determined stride toward the elevators.

To my chagrin, Deitz wasn't in the ice room. What if he was chasing the killer? Maybe I should call him after all. No. That might put him in danger. I had to trust that he'd be okay and wait for him to contact me. Decision made, I pressed the down button and waited with a churning stomach for the car to arrive at my floor.

By the time we reached the lobby, the elevator had stopped on every floor and I'd had to pick Shakes up so he wouldn't get stepped on. A few of our elevator companions fussed over the Pomeranian Devil, declaring how adorable he was, but the conversation mostly ran to speculation about the murder and the earlier shooting.

"I can't believe they're letting the lecture continue," one young woman said, her brown gaze doubtful.

"I heard they had every cop in the city here."

"But why wouldn't they just cancel the convention and send us all home?" an attractive older woman asked. "It's not like this is world-changing work we're doing here."

There was general chuckling at that. I joined in, because she was right. I believed in my profession. I believed it could be a powerful tool for helping families deal with their grief. But I'd never assumed we were important enough to be uncancellable.

"I don't think you're looking at this the right way," the older woman's companion said. He looked to be in his mid- to late thirties and had the bulky, fit form of someone who was ex-military. "The cops can't really let us all go. The killer is in this hotel. He probably thought the shooting would panic the cops into releasing everybody for safety reasons."

Heads nodded. The guy was right.

"That's why they locked everybody down," somebody near the doors said. "To protect us."

"But that also kept the killer out of sight," Mr. Potentially Ex-Military said. "So, they're opening things back up."

"Risky," I murmured before I realized I'd spoken it out loud.

Ex-Military nodded. "It is. But they're kind of in a bind."

The doors opened and we all stepped out. The lobby was abuzz, everyone seemingly torn between fear and excitement.

I scanned the lobby and saw that the police presence was heavy, and every cop was on high alert, intense gazes constantly sliding around the space. Shakes and I joined the stream of people heading into the lecture room, where two employees held out clipboards and asked each of us to sign the sheet of paper clipped there. Scanning the sheet quickly, I realized it was a waver against holding the hotel liable if anything happened. Those who wouldn't sign the waivers were sent back to their rooms.

I signed the form, knowing I'd rather be down there than locked in my room. I took an aisle seat in the center of the room. Shakes sat happily on my lap, his black button eyes scanning the area, probably looking for food.

Ten minutes later, the buzz in the room started to quiet as a tall, dark-haired man wearing a white, round-necked silk tee and charcoal slacks approached the dais at the front of the big room. He climbed the three, shallow steps on the side and moved with a languid grace toward the podium. The microphone gave a shrill squeal as he leaned slightly forward, lush lips seeming to kiss the strident thing as he began to speak.

He halted at the annoying feedback, his perfect mouth curving in a self-deprecating smile.

I could almost hear every woman in the place sighing with pleasure.

The man tapped the microphone with long, well-manicured fingers and began to speak. "Good morning. I'm Dr. Peter Steel." He hesitated, his smoldering gaze sliding over the crowd. As it skimmed over me, I could swear I felt a warm awareness sliding through my stomach. "And before all of you hypochondriacs get excited about getting free medical advice..."

The room erupted in appreciative laughter. I looked around, discovering that the men in the room seemed nearly as enchanted by the charming speaker as the women.

"I'm not *that* kind of doctor." He waggled dark brown brows, earning another wave of laughter from the crowd.

"My doctorate is in the therapy sciences. Specifically, grief therapy."

A delighted murmuring sifted through the crowd. I joined my colleagues in their fascination for that particular subject. A little-known fact in the professional mourner business is that, although what we do is considered to be an art form, there is considerable science involved as well. In order for us to meet our clients' full grieving needs, we needed to first understand the behavioral stresses behind those needs.

"...studies have shown that cognitive behavioral therapy, or CBT, is great for reducing the symptoms of depression and giving the patient safe, healthy ways of dealing with them. I'm happy to say that your employers and the organizers of this convention have recognized the value in this type of science in support of the clients they serve."

A sudden burst of laughter interrupted Dr. Steel's presentation. A brief flash of irritation crossed his perfect features and slid away as he saw the cause of the hilarity.

A woman leaned over the side of the coffin she'd been lying in, a dopy grin on her rumpled map of a heavily made-up face. When she saw him looking at her, Pinella grinned widely, giving him a little finger wave. "Hello, gorgeous!"

The room erupted again.

To his credit, Dr. Steel leaned on the podium and presented my elderly neighbor with the full force of his considerable charm. "Well, hello, young lady. I believe you've rushed the whole coffin experience. I'm pretty sure you should be a lot less mobile when you enter one of those."

The room roared with appreciation. But Pinella was not to be outdone. She nodded enthusiastically. "I was well and truly gone until you walked into my life," she told him with a wink. "But when I heard your sexy voice, it yanked me right back to life."

His laughter was infectious and not in the least affected. He glanced at the crowd, straightening to lift his hands, palms up. "Maybe I've got more of that type of doctor in me than I realized. It appears I've cured this woman of whatever ailed her."

More laughter.

Pinella sat upright in her pillowed death bed, enthusiastically shaking her head.

Steel noticed. "No? I haven't cured you?"

She winked at the crowd...ever the ham. "There's only one cure for what's ailing me, gorgeous. And you're gonna have to get a lot closer to perform it."

Wolf whistles filled the room, everyone enjoying Pinella's bawdy banter and Steel's good-natured reaction.

He actually blushed, but he descended the dais and strode over to Pinella, whose face was equally pink as he lifted one of her hands and gave it a kiss worthy of a romance novel cover to a thunderous roar of approval and pleasure.

He leaned close and whispered something in Pinella's ear and she nodded, turning and disappearing from sight for just a beat before reappearing on the other side of the coffin. We'd discovered after the first day trying to shove her into the casket, that the display coffins had special, hidden doors on the sides so the actors playing corpses could easily climb in and out of them.

If there'd been training for Pinella's coffin surfing job, she clearly hadn't taken it.

Steel offered her his arm and escorted her to a seat in the front row.

I couldn't stop grinning as I watched my neighbor take

up bubbling conversations with those around her. Pinella had earned the attention and was making the most of it.

Back behind the podium, Steel looked down on his biggest fan and grinned. Leaning into the microphone, he said, "Note to self. I need to add raising convention attendees from the dead to my resume."

Appreciative chuckles slid through the crowd. Shakes yipped happily, his fan of a tail smacking me in the face as he stood to show his support of whatever was causing the general hilarity. I realized the room was a lot more crowded than it had been when the lecture started. Turning half around in my seat, I noted a dozen or so hotel employees standing along the back wall, laughing and clapping along with the attendees.

Despite having a name like a second-rate porn star, Dr. Peter Steel was a resounding success. But, more importantly, he was the perfect distraction from an event that had turned deadly before it had really even had a chance to start.

"All right," Steel said, squaring his broad shoulders. "Let's get started, shall we?"

"Is this the first time you've heard Doctor Steel speak?" the woman next to me asked in a breathy whisper.

I turned to her and smiled. "Yeah. He's good."

She nodded enthusiastically as the crowd erupted into laughter at something Steel had said. "He's very popular with the ladies especially. Sometimes too popular, if you know what I mean."

Did I? I thought maybe I did. "Are you saying he seduces the attendees?"

"Seduce would be the wrong word," she said, lowering her voice and leaning closer. "He doesn't really need to seduce them. They pretty much throw themselves at him."

I thought about that for a beat. Was it possible Steel

seduced the victim and an enraged husband or lover took his anger too far? I turned to the woman next to me. "Do you know if he's seduced anyone here?"

She laughed softly. "Why? Are you going to offer yourself up for the task?"

I forced an answering chuckle. "Maybe."

She shook her head. "I haven't seen him with anyone." She slid a speculative gaze toward the spot where the dead woman had been found. "But I've had the same thought."

"You think he might have slept with the dead woman?"

"Angeline?" She shrugged again. "It's crossed my mind. Angel had..." she winced. "I guess you'd call it self-esteem problems. A guy like Steel would recognize the weakness and be perfectly capable of taking advantage of it."

I fixed the man at the podium with a look, trying to see him in the light of a serial seducer. It wasn't hard to imagine. Doctor Steel looked perfectly at home behind a podium. He seemed very comfortable with his subject matter and with speaking in front of a large crowd. He was a man who liked himself. Maybe too much? Turning back to the woman next to me, I asked, "How well did you know Angeline?"

"We've shared a few meals together at conferences. She was a nice person. But she never seemed comfortable in her own skin. And I got the feeling she was always looking for ways to cope with that."

"How so?"

"Drinking. Flirting. Occasionally she'd take drugs. The last conference where I ran into her, she was a mess. A woman's diamond necklace went missing. The cleaning staff was accused of stealing it. One little girl in particular took a lot of heat and ended up being fired over it. Angeline laughed about her losing her job. She and I actually had words over it. Then, the next day, it was as if she'd forgotten all about it."

I frowned. "It does sound as if she had some emotional issues. Was she married?"

"Not that I know of. She didn't wear a ring, anyway."

That seemed to destroy my theory of a wronged husband. But there could still be a lover. "Have you seen her with any other men since she's been here?"

"No. But I didn't really see her before this morning. I ran into her about five in the morning. She was getting a coffee from the lobby."

"You were in the lobby at five o'clock?" My tone was incredulous. "On purpose?"

She laughed. "That's actually how Angeline and I met. We both have...had..." She frowned. "trouble sleeping."

"Will you two take your conversation out to the lobby, please?" an angry woman behind us whispered.

I turned and said, "Sorry," and gave the other woman an embarrassed smile. I probably could have learned some interesting things from Dr. Peter Steel. But I was too busy with thoughts of the woman named Angeline. And the man who'd probably killed her.

8

"Why do you think a man killed her?" Argh asked, his judgmental gray gaze peering intently at me from across the high-top table in the hotel bar. The room was non-descript, looking like a thousand other hotel bars, with dark burgundy leather booths, dark walnut tables, and charcoal gray carpeting that hid the array of crumbs and spilled wine stains I was sure were there. Forest green metal pool-table style lights hung over the densely-packed area of high-top tables in the center and smaller green-glass lights hung on the wall over each booth. By contrast, the brightly-lit bar was like a beacon to customers in all that darkness, and the attractive bartenders added to its draw.

"It could as easily have been a woman," my brother added.

I nodded. "It could. Except that, as you well know, it's unusual for a woman to kill with a knife."

"Unusual, but not unheard of."

I sipped my wine, a crisp, cold Riesling that was already going to my head a little bit. In my lap, Shakes squiggled uncomfortably. He preferred a booth bench where he could stretch his tiny form or, more realistically, wedge his tiny nose into cracks looking for crumbs. Unfortunately, all the booths had been taken. The bar was hopping, and I wondered if the convention atmosphere was finally over-riding the dampening effects of the murder and the shooting.

Argh sighed. "It might not matter, anyway. It's possible our killer has fled the coop."

"Really?" I asked, surprised.

"Yeah. Someone reported seeing a tall man dressed in a hoodie escaping through the front doors right after the shooting. The police were in recovery mode for a few seconds. It was probably just enough time for our guy to slip outside virtually unnoticed."

My eyes went wide. "Does that mean we're all safe?"

"Possibly. But I'm staying here with a security detail just in case."

I glanced at my watch and frowned. I hadn't heard from Eddie since we'd parted on the fifth floor earlier.

"What's wrong?" Argh asked. His intense cop stare never missed a beat. "Where's your annoying sidekick?"

"Which one? Pinella or Eddie?"

"Either one. It seems you've been deserted."

I jerked my head toward a large booth in the back. Pinella and several other women sat with Doctor Peter Steel, seemingly having the time of their lives if all the cackling was any indication. "Pinella's over there flirting with one of the lecturers. Deitz is..." I frowned again.

Argh's antennae rose almost visibly. "What's he doing, MayBell? He'd better not be interfering in police business."

"He's not!" I declared. "Eddie wouldn't..."

Argh held up a hand and stood, throwing a twenty on

the table for our drinks. "Don't finish that sentence. As far as I can tell, you haven't lied to me in the last hour. Let's keep the streak going for a while longer."

I fought the urge to stick out my tongue. It wouldn't be very adult of me. Besides, the big guy at the next table over had just sneezed. There were sneeze spores dancing through the air. "I never lie," I lied.

Argh shrugged. "Okay. If you're not worried about the fact that he's missing..."

He turned and strode toward the door leading to the lobby. I fought an almost overwhelming urge to run after him and ask him to help me search for my lost boyfriend. But I couldn't do it. Not only would he be smug about it, but he'd take great pleasure in arresting Deitz for interfering in something the police didn't even seem interested in.

"Would you like to join us for a drink?" the guy who'd poisoned the air with his spit spores asked.

I skimmed him a look and forced what I hoped was a pleasant smile. After all, it wasn't his fault I was feeling cranky. "No. But thank you. I need to go." Scooping Shakes into my arms, I slipped quickly from the stool and waved at Pinella. She and the other women had their heads together and they all looked well-oiled. But they appeared to have temporarily lost the object of their mass desire.

I hurried toward the door. Heading for the stairs, I decided I'd check in at the fifth-floor ice room and, if Eddie wasn't there, I'd take the path he'd indicated he was going to take in following our target. Maybe the killer had done exactly as Deitz had thought he would. Possibly Eddie had followed him to the underground parking lot.

And maybe the killer had gotten one over on Deitz.

It was possible my boyfriend was lying on the cold, filthy concrete, one breath away from death. The thought had me hurrying toward the stairwell door, my heart pounding hard enough to make me dizzy.

I dove through and all but ran up the first level of steps, turning to take the next short rise of steps to the second floor. I was panting by the time I hit the fifth floor and yanked open the door. I set Shakes down and he immediately started to growl, his gaze on an open door halfway down the hallway.

My room!

I shushed Shakes and started toward the door, my gaze on a swivel. A hairdryer kicked on behind the door we were passing and I jumped with a yelp.

Shakes yelped too, probably because I'd caught the tip of his tiny foot under my boot when I'd jumped. A door at the far end of the hallway opened and a man shoved a room service tray outside before ducking back into the room.

There was no sign of the police officer I'd seen before. The door I was heading for yawned wide, the room behind it silent. I sidled up to the opening and looked into the room from beside it. I felt silly, knowing I'd been watching too many crime shows on television, but that open door told me something was very wrong.

When nobody shot at me, I leaned further into the door. "Eddie?"

Nothing.

Shakes growled softly, his tail whipping the air.

"Okay," I said quietly. "We'll go inside. Make sure you warn me if you see or hear anything. Okay?"

Shakes yipped and trotted forward, pulling his leash from my fingers before I realized he was moving. I hurried after him, calling his name in harsh whispers. "Shakes! Come back here right now!"

He ignored me as usual. I huffed out a frustrated sigh,

hurrying after him. My gaze slipped over the entire room. My suitcase looked untouched, messy just as I'd left it. My nightgown was still draped over the unmade bed next to a damp towel. A naked pillow lay on the floor next to the bed, giving me a moment's hesitation. Shaking it off, I quickly searched the bathroom, finding it empty, the shower mercifully body free.

Shakes gave a single short, sharp bark of recognition and I hurried around the king-sized bed. "Eddie?"

A soft scuff. A sharp intake of breath. I was distracted by the sight of my boyfriend face down on the carpet, blood clotting his hair.

I shouldn't have let myself get distracted.

Something was yanked over my head and jerked tight around my throat. I sucked in a breath and inhaled soft fabric. I tried to scream as a hard arm wrapped around my throat and dragged me backward, choking me.

I was dimly aware of Shakes snarling and dancing around my flailing feet. My attacker kicked out at the little dog but mercifully missed. Keeping me in between him and my dog, the man lowered his lips to the pillow case near my ear. A husky voice whispered, "Stay out of this or somebody else is going to die." Then he shoved me hard. I hit the wall and slipped to the floor, Shakes standing near my head and barking a warning.

But the door slammed shut and I knew, even before I pulled the pillowcase off my head, that he was gone. Still, I shoved to my feet and lurched clumsily toward the door, flinging it open.

The hallway was empty.

The phone in my room rang. I hurried toward it, forgetting about the call when Eddie groaned. I dropped to my knees next to him. "Eddie!"

His eyes came slowly open and he groaned, holding his head. "What hit me?"

"If I'm not mistaken, it was our killer," I said, helping him lift his head and shoving a pillow under it. "Just lie there for a minute. It looks like he hit you with something." The bottle of wine I'd brought with me to the convention lay on its side nearby, blood smearing the label. "I'm guessing that's what he hit you with."

"How in the world did you get into my room?"

Rubbing a hand over his temple, he sighed. "I saw someone break into it and followed him."

Hope filled me. "You saw our killer?"

"Unfortunately not. He wore a surgical-type mask over the lower part of his face and had one of those stretchy hats pulled down over his hair. He moved fast. I didn't get a good look at him before he ducked into the room." He frowned. "I was careful, but the guy must have been hiding in the closet. I was barely through the door before he attacked."

I told Deitz what the attacker had said to me as his head cleared. "It sounds as if he doesn't want to kill anybody else," I said, frowning.

That would explain why I hadn't seen him either. I hadn't checked the closet yet when I realized Eddie was hurt and forgot about searching.

"Judging by the percussion band playing in my skull, he certainly doesn't mind *hurting* people," Eddie snarked. He sat up, groaning softly. "I can't believe I let him sneak up on me."

I laughed. "Join the club. This guy's good at sneaking around."

My phone rang again. I sighed. "Let me get this. Somebody really wants to talk to me." Sitting on the edge of the bed, I grabbed the phone. "Hello?"

"Hi. Is this May Ferth?"

I frowned, not recognizing the voice. "Yes. Who's this?"

"I'm Veronica."

I sat through a moment of ensuing silence, unsure what I was supposed to say. I didn't know any Veronica. "I'm sorry..."

"Oh. Dang! Sorry. I sat next to you at Doctor Steel's lecture earlier? We chatted."

"Yes," I said hesitantly. "Hi. Um. How did you...?"

"The older lady gave me your name. Pruella? Pinwheel? That's not right, but it was something like that."

"Pinella. She's my neighbor."

"Right. She told me that. Can we meet somewhere private?"

I glanced at Eddie. "Can you come to my room?"

"That would be perfect. What's your room?"

I gave her the number.

"I'll be there in five minutes."

I was watching for her when she stepped off the elevator and hurried down the hall toward me. I didn't know why, but I had a feeling she was in danger and watching for her seemed like a good idea.

The woman smiled when she saw me waiting. "Thanks so much for letting me come up. I didn't know what else to do."

I stepped into the room. Veronica entered and jerked to a stop when she saw Deitz. Her entire body went stiff.

"It's okay," I told her. "That's Eddie. He's my boyfriend."

"Can you...?" she swallowed hard. "Do you know for sure he's not..."

Eddie mopped at the blood on his face. "I'm pretty sure the guy we're looking for just hit me over the head. I'm firmly on your side in this. Trust me."

She looked at me and I nodded my agreement. "It's definitely not Eddie."

Eddie moved around us and went to the bathroom to tend to his wound and give us privacy. I motioned toward the small couch under the window. "Sit. Would you like something? I have wine, water, and chocolate." I wasn't sure why I'd brought a Halloween-sized bag of miniature candy bars to the convention, but several people had told me it was a good idea. So far, all it had gotten me was about three extra pounds because I tended to eat when I was stressed.

"I'll take a bottle of water. Thanks."

I gave her the water and pulled the bag of candy out of my suitcase, offering it to her. She plucked out a peanut butter cup and a nut and caramel bar. "Thanks. With everything that's been going on, I forgot to eat lunch."

"I've pretty much been living on wine and chocolate myself," I told her, smiling.

She laughed. "If anyone had told me that's how it was, I'd have signed up for more conventions." She frowned, her thoughts turning inward.

"Are you okay?" I asked Veronica. "Has someone hurt you?"

She blinked and her gaze refocused. "Sorry. I didn't sleep very well last night. My mind's racing." The woman shook her head. "I'm okay. I realized after we spoke though, that I might have seen something which could be important."

"Something about the murder?" I asked.

Veronica nodded. "I saw Angeline arguing with someone." Her frown deepened. "It was a pretty bad fight. He had her pressed against the wall in the back hallway, near the hotel offices."

"Was he threatening her?" I asked.

"His body language was aggressive. And he's a big guy. She was the color of paper and looked terrified."

"Did you tell anyone?" Eddie asked.

Veronica flushed. "I should have. I know that now. But…" Tears filled her eyes. "I guess I bought into the rumors about her. She was something of a party girl. Sometimes when you're casual with other people's feelings, there's push back." She sniffed, her eyes glistening with unshed tears. "If I'd known."

"What happened with the argument," I asked, pulling her away from her guilty musings. She'd have to deal with what happened in her own way. But at the moment it was important for us to find the killer.

"Angeline shoved him in the chest and walked away. The last I saw of him, he was stalking in the opposite direction."

"Can you describe the guy?" Eddie asked.

"I can do better than that," Veronica said, some of the color leeching from her overheated face. "I can tell you his name. He works for the hotel. He's one of the security guards."

9

Veronica was right. Jessie Marks was definitely a big guy. I put him at about six five and two hundred and fifty pounds. Most of that was muscle. He'd been overseeing the security team for the hotel and had to be paged when Eddie and I asked for him.

Marks frowned when he saw us standing by the front desk, his gaze skimming toward the main entrance as if he were considering making a run for it.

Eddie strode toward the other man, a disarming smile on his face. Stretching out one hand, he pulled his credentials from his pocket with the other. "Mr. Marks. I'm Eddie Deitz. I'm working with the police trying to locate our shooter. How are you today?"

Marks' response was to slide a deep-set brown gaze over me and tighten his jaw. A muscle in his cheek jumped and he stood with his hands slightly raised, gunslinger style. "What can I help you with, Mr. Deitz?"

"We understand you knew the victim?"

The man blinked in surprise. "Angeline?" His expression tightened and he glanced away. "I knew her. We went out a few times." His eyes glistened and I realized they held unshed tears. "We weren't seeing each other anymore."

"You broke up?" I asked.

He looked down at Shakes. "That your dog?" he asked instead of answering my question. When I nodded, he asked, "He friendly?"

"He is," I responded, wondering if Marks was coping the best way he knew how. He was a strong guy. Probably a bit of an Alpha male. He wouldn't want to cry.

The security guard crouched down and placed a big hand on either side of Shakes' fuzzy head, rubbing the little dog's tiny, perked ears with his thumbs. "He's a nice dog. Sometimes we get these little yippers in the hotel and they're pains in the...um...backside." He gave me an apologetic look. "What's his name?"

"Shakespeare."

He mouthed the name silently, then smiled. "Cute. You're one of the actors from the convention?"

I felt Eddie shift and placed a hand on his arm. Knowing him as I did, I knew he was about to try to wrangle Marks back to the subject at hand. Something told me that would be a mistake. The man would tell us what he knew. But he'd do it in his own way. In his own time.

Marks scooped Shakes up and stood, holding him close. I recognized that my dog was his buffer to the trauma of what he was going to tell us and didn't object. "Me and Angeline fought. I said some mean things that I regretted as soon as I said them." The tears slipped down his stubbled cheek. "I hurt her feelings. I could tell I did." He didn't seem to realize what the confession meant for him. "I'll always have to live with that now."

"If you don't mind," Eddie said softly. "Can you tell us what you fought about?"

Marks held Shakes against his chest with one big hand, his pointer finger scratching my dog's tiny chest. "The rumors about Angeline weren't true. Yeah, she liked to party. Who doesn't?"

I gave him a non-committal look, embarrassed to admit that I didn't like to party. I never had. I was pretty much a homebody who loved her dog and her family and going to work at a job I enjoyed. I felt little need to drink or do any peopling outside of work.

"She didn't pick guys up everywhere she went. If anything, they tried to pick her up."

I nodded because he'd fixed me with an earnest look that seemed to need a response.

"Had someone tried to pick her up recently?" Eddie asked. "Is that why you fought?"

Marks glared at Deitz. "I wouldn't get mad at her for that. What kind of a jerk do you think I am?"

"I don't know what kind of man you are, Mr. Marks. That's why I'm asking."

Marks sighed. "You're right. I'm sorry. I have a temper. It's always been a problem. But I never lost it with her before. Angeline was so kind and sweet." His expression soured. "But she shouldn't have blown me off like that. She shouldn't have disrespected me."

Shakes whined softly and I reached to take him back. "Tell us exactly what happened," I said, my tone kind but firm. "We're trying to help," I added when he hesitated.

A moment passed before he spoke. Eddie and I let the silence build, knowing the first one to speak would lose the upper hand. Finally, he sighed. "We were going out to dinner. Frankie's Place, down on 5th and Voorhees. It's where we went the first time we went out. It's special to us." He frowned. "It meant a lot to me anyway. Now, I'm not sure how Angeline felt about it."

"She didn't make it to your date?" Deitz asked.

Marks barked out a bitter-sounding laugh. "She didn't even let me know she was making other plans."

"What plans?" I asked.

He shook his head. "She insisted it was innocent. Just two colleagues having a couple of drinks to talk about work. Apparently, the colleague was having some kind of crisis he needed her help with."

The way he said it told me better than words what he thought of that. "You don't believe he had a crisis?"

"He probably thought he did. I'm sure his crisis had more to do with getting Angeline alone than anything else."

"You believe she had another date, so she blew you off?" Deitz asked.

I flinched at the strong characterization, but Marks didn't seem to take offense. "I *know* she blew me off. Whether she saw it as a date or a work thing I couldn't tell you. All I..." His voice broke and the hand he scrubbed over his mouth was shaking. "All I know is that I'll never hear her beautiful voice or touch her silky skin again."

"Do you have any idea who the man was, Mr. Marks?" Deitz asked.

"Angeline said he had something to do with the convention. That's all she would tell me about him." He gave a bitter laugh. "It was like she thought I was going to punch him or something."

"Would you have?" When he looked at me, I clarified. "Punched him?"

Marks shook his head, but he didn't answer my question. His eyes were shiny with fresh tears.

"Mr. Marks, did you kill Angeline Porter?"

Marks seemed to deflate, his broad shoulders folding inward and his face turning gray. Tears fell unheeded down his saggy cheeks. "No. I could never hurt Angeline. I'd die if I did."

Eddie and I said our goodbyes with a warning not to leave town. I felt self-conscious telling the man that. We weren't cops. It wasn't as if we had anything to back it up with. But Marks simply nodded, no longer looking like a man who was thinking about making a run for it.

"I don't think he killed her," I told Eddie as soon as we were far enough away.

Eddie didn't respond. He had a thoughtful look on his face that told me he was considering something.

"What?" I asked. I had to ask him a second time before I got his attention. "Eddie?"

"I was just thinking it's pretty convenient that Marks was seen fighting with the victim before she was killed. The man's either very unlucky..."

"Or someone set him up." I thought about that for a beat. "Either way, it's so sad for him."

Eddie reached out and clasped my hand, squeezing it gently and holding on tight. "Yeah."

"Where to now?" I asked.

Deitz turned to look at the front desk. "Do you know who organized the convention?"

"Not by name, no. But I'll bet the hotel would know. There would have to be an interface between the event and the hotel."

"Good. Let's go talk to them."

"Let me guess," said a hostile voice behind us. "You've been busily sticking your noses into police business."

I turned to find Argh striding toward us, an unhappy

look on his face. "And *you're* busy ruining everybody's day," I countered.

He seemed to give that some thought, then nodded. "Actually, yes." He stopped in front of us and sighed. "I hate to admit it, but I need your help."

My eyes went wide. I cupped one of my ears with a hand. "Eh? What's that? I'm sure I didn't hear you right."

An intense gray gaze scoured over me, leaving prickles of warning behind. "You heard me, MayNever. I'm bumping up against something of a barrier and I need your help to get around it."

"Nobody will talk to you," Eddie surmised.

Argh's lips thinned. "You'd think the hotel was filled with turtles and I was a curious dog. Everybody takes one look at me and retreats into their shells."

"What is it exactly you want from me?" I asked my frustrated brother.

"I want you to do what you do best."

I arched a brow. "You want me to annoy you until you run away shrieking?"

"No, Maykbelieve. I want you to be a professional mourner. After all, you're always telling me it's a calling and that you're good at it."

I bristled. "I am good at it."

"Perfect. Then you won't mind doing some professional mourning for me."

"What in the world are you talking about?" I asked my brother. "Have you been sniffing glue again?"

He rolled his eyes. "I did that once, May. Once. I was four years old. You need to let that go."

I grinned at Eddie. "You should have seen him. He was yelling at a squirrel in the back yard, asking it why it was pink. It was hilarious."

"Yeah, hilarious. I was the only kid in pre-school who had to tape all my art projects together because mom told them never to let me have glue."

I snorted out a laugh. Eddie's lips twitched.

"It was like they thought I was a glue addict or something. One time, May. Once."

I was laughing so hard that tears slipped down my cheeks and I was having trouble breathing.

Argh crossed his arms over his chest and glared at me. "Can we move on, please?"

I hiccupped and nodded. "Carry on, glue-snorter."

"Jeezopete," Argh mumbled. He fixed Eddie with a frustrated look. "You're an only child, right?"

Eddie gave up trying not to smile. "Thankfully."

Inclining his head, Argh said, "Lucky sap."

I slammed my lips closed on a particularly hefty hiccup and covered my mouth. "Okay. I'm done entertaining myself at your expense. Tell me what you have in mind."

"You'll help?"

"Maybe. Talk."

"We want to do a viewing for Angeline."

I stared at him for a beat, wondering if I should search his pockets for a glue pen.

"What?" he asked. "It wasn't my idea. But I think it could work."

"Work how?" Eddie asked.

"The killer will definitely show up. They just can't resist. Once here, he might let down his hair, thinking he's gotten away with murder. With any luck and some careful misinformation to stick in his craw, he might make a mistake."

"An interesting idea," I admitted.

"Then you'll do it?" he asked.

I thought about it for a beat and then nodded. "As long as Pinella isn't the one in the coffin."

Argh's gaze slid guiltily away.

"Noooo," I whined. "You know she's going to rise from the dead again, right? The zombies on that Traveling Dead show move less than she does when she's supposed to be acting like a corpse."

"I love that show," Argh said, grinning. "Don't worry. I've given her strict instructions."

"And what did she say when you told her she had to lie still and not talk?"

His smile died. "It's going to be fine, May."

"What did she say?" I pushed.

Argh expelled air. "She said not to worry. She's got the whole corpse thing down. And besides, only vampires and zombies rise from the dead and she didn't have the right clothes for either of those gigs."

Deitz barked out a laugh. "That sounds about right."

"Who's going to play the grieving significant other?" I asked, sighing.

"You probably don't want to use anybody from the convention." Deitz told my brother. "There's a good chance she's dated most of the men, which will surely start a fist fight or two, and I doubt her proclivities made her particularly popular with the women."

Argh nodded. "I've got that covered too," he said. It will be fine."

"Not even the hotel staff is safe," I told him. "She dated one of the security guards."

Argh nodded impatiently. "Trust me. I've got it. And don't worry. The role is not going to be for a lover. He's going to play a relative."

"It needs to be an outsider," I warned.

"MayBee, stop buzzing. I've got this…"

"Who…?" I challenged.

Argh grinned at someone over my shoulder. That grin turned my blood cold. "Argh…?"

"It's going to be great," my brother said smugly.

"I doubt it," said Eddie, grimacing.

I couldn't look. "Let me guess…"

"Dude!"

Sweet Carolina in an ice storm…

10

I whipped around, not believing my own ears. My mostly monosyllabic neighbor drifted toward me in a residual cloud of marijuana smoke. He lifted a hand in a friendly wave. "Dude," he said fondly.

I turned to my brother, arching a dark-blonde brow in question.

Ignoring me, Argh nodded at Doug and offered him his hand. "Thanks for coming, Doug. Are you ready to get started?"

"Argh," I said, my tone filled with frustration. "Talk to me. Why are you dragging Doug into this?"

"Dude," my neighbor said, clearly disappointed in me.

I shook my head. "I know you're happy to help, Doug," I told him. "But this deal is dangerous. I already have to worry about Pinella. I have no idea why my brother thought it was a good idea to drag you into this too."

"Pinella's here?" Doug asked, his shaggy brows lifting.

"She's working as a corpse," Eddie told Doug.

Even with his mind perpetually mellowed by his legal drug habit, Doug winced at that. "Dude."

I nodded in complete agreement. "Talk, Argh."

He glanced at his watch. "You said it yourself, May. The grieving person needs to be an outsider. Doug's perfect."

Perfect? My brother needed to consult a dictionary to revisit what that word meant. I opened my mouth to argue, but was distracted by a chiming sound. Glancing at my phone, I was surprised to see a general call to gather in the main lecture room. "What's this about?" I asked no one in particular.

"It's about finding a killer," Argh said.

THE ROOM WENT EERILY quiet as a man I'd never met before walked to the podium. I didn't know who he was, but there was something strangely familiar about him. I was pretty sure I'd seen him someplace before, but I couldn't place where.

The man was about six feet tall, maybe just under that, it was hard to tell as he stepped up on the podium. His hair was sand-colored and straight, combed neatly to one side in a no-frills, no-nonsense way. His eyes appeared dark in the harsh lighting, but I couldn't tell what color they were.

Something about the taut way he held himself. The iron set to his square jaw. Struck a memory deep inside my mind.

"Hello. I'm Joshua Barnford. As many of you probably know, my company, Barnford Events, is sponsoring this convention. Welcome to Mourning Con."

Unenergetic applause followed.

Barnford gave us an equally lethargic smile. "And thank you for hanging with us through the...difficulties."

Murmurs rippled through the large room, expressions filled with a mix of anger, confusion, and fear.

Barnford plowed ahead as if he hadn't noticed. "Due to the unique nature of this event and its attendees, I've been given a rare request. After much discussion and deliberation, I've made the decision to grant the request. As you know, industry vendors will arrive in the morning and discussion sessions will begin. But for today the event will be given over to celebrating the life of Angeline Porter. And mourning her death in the particular way you're all so good at."

The room exploded with outrage.

"I can't believe..."

"That's outrageous!"

"Are you kidding me?"

Barnford held up his hand. "Please." He looked around the room, lowering his hand to indicate the room should quiet. When his voice could be heard again, he went on. "This is not what you think it is. I received a request directly from Angeline's family to honor her memory in a way she would have loved. Angeline was proud of her profession. She was very good at it. And her brother believes she would be pleased to know she had one last part to play."

More rumblings. But emotions seemed to have calmed.

"Think of it as a way to say goodbye to someone who, even if you didn't personally know her, shared your passion for helping people at their most vulnerable, difficult time. As well as your unique skillset. One that few others could understand."

He stood and let the murmurs roll over him, his expression serene and his posture relaxed.

"Please tell me you're not going to put her in a casket for everyone to ogle?"

I recognized Jessie Marks' agonized voice.

Barnford shifted his gaze to the big man at the back of

the room. He shook his head. "Angeline will be with us in spirit only. I assure you, our only intent is to honor her by allowing her to inspire one last professional mourning gig. So, what do you all say? Will you join us in giving Angeline one last professional mourning job?"

For a few tense seconds, people sat perfectly still, seemingly unsure what to do. But then a woman in the front row stood. Followed a beat later by a man in the center aisle. Then three more people. And then five more. And soon most of the room was standing.

I glanced at Deitz and he nodded, standing up and heading toward the exit. He would report to my brother that our sting was a go.

Wishing I felt better about that, I shivered as I scanned a look around the room. I couldn't help wondering which of the people in there with me had killed a woman and then threatened Eddie and me and all my friends. With a sense of coming doom, I sighed. We'd find out who it was soon enough.

"WHERE'S ARGH?" I asked my boyfriend as I exited the lecture room. Rather than responding, he clasped my elbow and put some distance between us and the exiting mass of people.

When we were far enough away from the crowd, he lowered his voice and spoke into my ear. "He got called away. Another murder across town. He left me in charge."

Ah. That explained why Deitz was being so secretive. For all intents and purposes, he'd be acting as a cop. But everybody knew him as my significant other. The assembled actors would believe he was playing a role as they were. The killer would hopefully feel the same.

Argh had been the weak point in the sting from the beginning. Some of the attendees had no doubt connected him with the police presence in the hotel. But he hadn't wanted to relinquish the role to anyone else, citing the danger and unpredictability of our situation.

"I don't like it," I told Eddie. "It's not safe."

He tilted my chin up and kissed me. It was a sweet kiss. A lingering one. And it made my belly dance with pleasure. When he broke the kiss, he reached for my hand. "I'll be fine. And I'll be glad to stay closer to you. Just in case."

I let him give me the happy talk because there was no way around it. The sting needed someone who knew how to handle himself if the killer came out of hiding and started playing dirty. I sighed. Unfortunately, the killer had already caught Deitz stalking him. I mentioned that, remembering the terror of finding Eddie bleeding on the rug in my room.

Eddie's response was to shake his head. "He doesn't know I was stalking him. I pretended to be looking for you. He was just taking care of a potential witness. It will be fine."

I doubted that. But it was what it was. "Okay. Let's go speak to Barnford and find out how he wants this to play out."

Joshua Barnford had wrangled an office for himself in the hotel. He was on his phone, sitting behind a tidy maple desk when we arrived, facing out into a non-descript hallway that fed off the lobby. The entire front wall of the office was glass and I watched him as we approached. The organizer looked tense, his expression dark. As we neared the office, he scrubbed a hand through his sand-colored hair and then leaned forward, pounding a fist on the desk as he snapped something to the person on the other end of the line.

Eddie knocked on the door and Barnford looked up, waving us inside. Quickly ending the call, he squelched his angry expression on a dime and gave us a confident smile. "There are my people of the hour."

Barnford stood and leaned across the desk, offering Eddie his hand. "Mr. Deitz, a pleasure. Detective Ferth told me you'd be my point of contact for security on this."

"I will. And you'll have additional security personnel standing by?"

"Out of sight but near enough to cut off the target's escape should that become necessary." He laughed, rubbing large, well-manicured hands together. "Target. I feel like I've stepped into a crime show on TV. I'll admit I was nonplussed when Detective Ferth came to me with the viewing suggestion. I've never really been introduced to the concept of professional mourning before this convention opportunity came up."

"Doesn't that make it hard to hold a convention for it?" Eddie asked.

"Not at all," Barnford said, shaking his head. "I engage knowledgeable experts whenever I design a convention. I've done cons for industries from party clowns to zoo keepers. I always learn fascinating things."

My smile felt forced. Probably because it was. But when the organizer focused his attention on me, I dug into my acting tool bag and turned the wattage up. "Well, we're not going to be on television, but it will be like a crime show."

He nodded. "Please, sit." Indicating two small chairs

across the desk, Barnford sat down again. "My under-standing is that we're going to do a faux viewing honoring the victim."

I nodded. "Purely theatrical. I'll be playing the grieving sister and Eddie will be portraying a security guard."

"Understood." Barnford said. "Are we going to portray the killer too?"

"No." I responded. "But we are going to try to draw the real killer out by offering false information he'll likely feel compelled to correct." I wasn't happy letting Barnford in on the ruse, but Argh had insisted he'd run a request for the man's criminal history record information and cleared him. According to my brother, Barnford's record was as clean as the wind-driven snow.

"Will that work?" Barnford asked, his expression guile-less. When he saw the look I sent him, he laughed. "Sorry. I'm just curious." He zipped his lips.

"It's a reasonable question," Eddie said. "Believe it or not, whatever the motivation that inspires a killer to kill, he or she usually has a sense of...not pride exactly but some-thing close. They don't want the act to be misunderstood or misrepresented. The urge to clarify is nearly impossible to resist."

Barnford shook his head. "People are fascinating."

"Yes," Eddie gave him a grim smile.

"I'll stay out of the way and wait for all to be revealed." Barnford stood. "If that's all?"

We stood too. "We just wanted to find out if you had any requests."

He shook his head. "I'll have my security people in plain clothes as waitstaff to ease any problems that arise. But otherwise, I'm assuming it's your show. My work begins in the morning when the vendors arrive."

I nodded.

"You received your scripts from Detective Ferth?" Barnford asked.

"We did."

"Then, I wish you both well." He shook our hands again. "Let's find this killer."

Rah, rah, I thought grimly.

11

The "Reverend" at Angeline's viewing was a man I'd chatted with the night before when we'd both been checking into the hotel. He looked genuine in black slacks, a black button up shirt, and a white collar. It was only if you looked too closely that you realized the "collar" was a white dinner napkin rolled and probably pinned beneath his shirt collar in the back.

Despite my desperate sobs, he approached Doug and me in silent black sneakers, his rosy face bearing a grief-laden expression for the sister and brother of the deceased. Holding out his hands, "Reverend" Miller took my fingers in his own, not even wincing at the moist tissue clutched in my palm. Being of the profession, he no doubt realized the tissue had only been dampened by fake tears from a small, white bottle. "I'm so sorry about your loss," he said, his voice perfectly pitched for mourning.

I nodded, sniffling, and lifted the tattered tissue to my eyes, too emotional to speak.

Beside me, Doug opened his mouth and I barely kept from wincing. His usual verbal shortcuts were not going to add much to the subdued mood of the room. I really didn't think just saying "Dude" to everyone who came to offer their condolences was going to cut it.

"Reverend," Doug said, his voice cultured and smooth. "Thank you for honoring our wishes. Aunt Angeline was very taken by you that summer in Boston when we chatted over cold beers and juicy bratwursts at the Hiller's home."

For a moment I forgot the script. I stared at my "brother" with my mouth hanging open while both men turned to me, expecting me to say my lines. I shook my head, swallowing hard, and winged it with a noisy sob instead.

Like a pro, Miller picked the conversation back up without hesitation. "I know this is a hard time for you," he said, his expression a picture-perfect mix of grief and understanding. "Your aunt was such a kind woman. Everybody loved her. She will surely be missed."

I sniffled loudly and nodded, patting my nose with the soggy tissue. "Thank you, Reverend. You were her favorite confidant at Trinity Lutheran Church. She always said you gave the best sermons."

"That's kind of you to say." Miller frowned. "There's something important I need to speak to you two about."

"Oh?" Doug asked, the picture of polite interest.

"Yes," Miller said. "Your aunt spoke to me about something worrying the last time I saw her..."

"Ah!!!"

We all jolted and turned just in time to see a young woman fold downward, apparently overcome by her grief. A man standing nearby caught her before she hit the ground, pulling her upright with a few murmured words.

"You were my favorite actress at the community theater," the woman said in a tear-filled voice to the body laid out in the casket. "I'll never forget your depiction of the zombie that one time." Her face went blank for a beat as she clearly tried to remember the name of the play. "I'm sorry," she sobbed out. "I can't remember the name of it. But you were the best zombie there. I *believed* you in the role. You know? I could almost picture your flesh sloughing off and green goo running down your face."

Tittering ensued around the actress and I saw her lips twitching as she fought a laugh. In an effort to overcome, she gave a violent shudder, leaning heavily on the man as he also fought not to smile. "I can't believe you're gone." She moaned, swaying on her feet. "I heard him threaten you. I knew you were in trouble. I should have said something." Her slender legs buckled again and she hit the ground, catching her companion by surprise. "It's all my fault," the woman intoned, folding into a sobbing mess on the floor.

Miller gave us a harried frown. "If you'll excuse me."

We nodded, watching him hurry across the room to address the young woman. Together with the man standing by her side, the three of them moved toward a bank of chairs that had been set out for mourners.

Deitz showed up a minute later and sat down next to her, giving me the first indication that the woman's final lines might have been unscripted.

"Dude!" Doug said, shaking his head.

"I have no idea," I told him. "I think her family wrote the script, weaving her real experiences into it. But, in their defense, it was a rush job."

He shook his dirty blond dread-head and clucked his tongue.

I was dying to tell Doug his portrayal had been inspired, but I never got the chance. A ruckus near the door had me turning to find Jessie Marks trying to shove his way into the room. When he saw me looking, he pointed an accusing finger in my direction. "You! This is all your fault. How dare you mock her? How dare you...!"

Eddie left the actress he'd been speaking to and pushed through the crowd, tugging Marks around to sever his gaze from mine. He leaned close, serving up an angry diatribe as Marks crossed beefy arms over his chest and glared back at my PI.

"Was that part of the script?" Doug asked sotto voce.

I shook my head. "Unfortunately, Mr. Marks doesn't think we should be doing this. He loved her." I didn't add that I wasn't sure either. It would serve no purpose since the decision hadn't been mine to make. I'd taken the role of Angeline's daughter in the mock viewing simply to ensure the whole affair was dignified and fair.

"Where's your furry little sidekick?"

Doug and I turned to find Peter Steel joining us. I gave him a wary smile. "I left him in my room. It's safer for him there."

Steel nodded toward the door and a retreating Jessie Marks. "That was an interesting turn of events, wasn't it? I take it Mr. Marks isn't a fan of this exercise?"

I fought an impulse to politely excuse myself. Something about Peter Steel rubbed me the wrong way. "It appears not," I finally said.

"He and the vic...Angeline Porter..." Doug corrected himself, "Were lovers?"

To my surprise, Steel nodded. "I'll admit that was not a pairing I would have predicted."

"Really?" That caught my interest. "Why not?"

Steel shrugged. "Angeline was..."

I expected him to classify her as a party girl as everyone else had. But he surprised me again.

"She was a joyful, fun-loving person. She enjoyed

making people laugh and smile. Whereas Mr. Marks is... intense is probably a good word. But maybe what they say about opposites attracting is true."

"I got the impression the romantic feelings were mostly on Mr. Marks' part," I offered. "From what Marks told us, Angeline was sometimes casual with her promises." That was a broad characterization of what Marks had told Eddie and me. But my gut told me it was right.

"That wouldn't surprise me. Many men...and some women..." he winked at me, "tried to wrangle a commitment from our Angeline. But she wasn't having it." He leaned close, lowering his voice conspiratorially. "Between us, I wouldn't be surprised to find out she had someone at home. A husband or wife. She approached these events like a vacation at an adult playground. Totally lacking in seriousness."

"What about you?" I asked Steel. "Did you try to wrangle a commitment from Angeline?"

His laugh was rich and pleasant, and brought more than one head around. "Angeline and I shared a love of romantic freedom. It's why we got along so well," he said, grinning.

"Did you?" I asked. "Or did you discover you wanted more from her and she wasn't willing to give it?"

His smile fell away. But it wasn't replaced by anger. He cocked his head like a curious bird. "You're asking me if I killed her."

I shrugged, my gaze holding his.

Doug had been looking around, to all appearances not following our conversation. But when Steel fell silent, my neighbor turned to him. "What exactly *was* your relationship with Angeline?"

Steel took the pseudo accusation in stride. "We were friends with benefits. Nothing more. I respected Angeline as a professional. I'd actually approached her with a business proposition. But she hadn't seemed interested in my proposal." He shrugged, seemingly not affected by her rejection. "Well, I must be off. I need to speak to the young woman over there about her heavy-handed style." He pointed to the woman whom Miller had gone to rescue from a bad case of overdoing it. "Thank heaven this wasn't a real viewing. There's still time to teach her something about the science of mourning."

Doug and I watched Steel stride confidently away. Doug spoke first. "He's just a little full of himself, isn't he?"

"He certainly is." I decided that was probably one of the reasons he rubbed me the wrong way.

"With an ego like that, he could certainly have taken Angeline's rejection of his business offer badly," Doug offered.

He was right. "It's certainly something worth considering." What I didn't say, but in all honesty could have, was that I wouldn't be bothered to learn Steel was our killer. There would be a certain rightness to that outcome.

I turned to Doug. "I'm running to the ladies' room. Will you stay near the coffin in case anybody wants to give their condolences?"

He gave me double thumbs up and moved closer to the silk-lined casket with the small, surprisingly quiet body in it.

I eyed the "corpse" seeing only the telltale zebra pattern of her tunic and the sparkle of a truly gaudy necklace with several ping-pong-ball sized orange glass gems. I was just glad I couldn't see the matching orange turban the "corpse" wore on her head. I caught Doug's eye and raised my brows. He nodded, giving me a thumbs up. Pinella was still among the living. Which, given the unnatural silence coming from the lipstick-smeared lips under the turban, told me she must be sleeping.

I stepped into the empty ladies' restroom with a sigh. Leaning against the door for a beat, I closed my eyes and savored the peace. Then, pushing guiltily away from the door, I went into the last stall to do my business. A moment later, The door opened again and two women entered, chattering excitedly.

"Honestly," said the first one. "It was really only a matter of time. That chick liked to play games. I've seen her around at a few cons and there was always drama around her."

"No, Heather," said a second voice. "This is different. She was crying in the bathroom last night. I tried to help her but all she would say was that she'd be okay as soon as she got out of this stupid place."

"I heard someone had threatened her job," the first woman said.

"Really? Who?"

I pictured the first woman shrugging.

"Someone who had the power to back it up. Angeline might have been a tease, but she *was* serious about her work. She loved being a pro. She'd die without it."

I flushed and stepped out of the stall, throwing the women a harmless smile. They'd gone silent and focused on applying lipstick and fluffing their hair when they'd realized I was there. I let the silence sit for a beat and then turned to them. "I'm really sorry. I could pretend I didn't hear what you said, but I did. Do you really think Angeline was being threatened by somebody?"

The women exchanged a look.

"I'm just curious, like you," I said. "It's not like I can do anything about it." *Unless they gave me something I could use.* I thought.

The older woman fluffed her dark hair and leaned back

against the counter. "It's true. I spoke to her myself. She was terrified of somebody."

Wanting to keep her at ease, I leaned toward the mirror and checked my teeth as if looking for an errant piece of salad. "She didn't tell you who it was?"

"Not in so many words."

I turned to her, giving her my full attention.

"All she'd say was that the person was smart and ruthless and threatened her livelihood."

"That could be anybody," the petite blonde who was with her said, looking disappointed. "If the police don't catch this guy, we're all in danger."

The dark-haired woman nodded. "They'll find him."

I didn't share her confidence. Maybe because one of those police, my brother, had set up the whole mock viewing because he was out of ideas for how to catch the guy. "She said he was smart, and ruthless?" I asked, hoping the woman would clarify.

Nodding, she said, "And had the ability to affect her job." She shook her head. "I have no idea what that means."

I had a couple of ideas. "Why do you think she mentioned his being smart?"

Dark Hair shrugged. "Maybe because the person she was talking about had been manipulating her and other people." As soon as the words came out of her perfectly made-up lips, her eyes went wide. "I'd forgotten that part." She covered her mouth. "She said this person really knew how to handle and control people. Those were almost her exact words."

I thought of Peter Steel, who was a self-described behaviorist and scientist. He'd certainly understand the human psyche enough to manipulate people. "Could it have been Doctor Steel?"

Both women blinked in surprise. The blonde laughed. "Peter? No way. He's a lover, not a killer."

Unless his skin was as thin as I thought it was. People who acted as confident as Steel did were generally not confident at all. And he certainly could have had an affair with Angeline, making her interest in Jessie Marks a point of contention between them. "Do you know if Steel and Angeline had a thing together?" I asked.

They both shrugged. Dark Hair said, "It's nearly a sure thing. They both liked to party and made themselves available." She frowned. "But I can't imagine he'd ever hurt her. They seemed like good friends."

"And he wouldn't have any control over her work," the blonde said as if that signified the end of my questioning. "Anyway..." she looked at the other woman. "We should get back."

I thanked them and watched them toddle out on four-inch heels, wishing I had their confidence that Peter Steel wasn't the killer. If only because that would eliminate one potential suspect. But I didn't share their surety about him. And I didn't know if it was because he rubbed me the wrong way. Or because he was genuinely innocent.

Sighing, I stepped out of the restroom and stopped, my gaze caught on the spot on the wall where bullet holes pocked the smooth surface.

The reality of my situation hit me then, like a rock between the eyes. My knees wobbled and I dropped onto the bench where I'd left Pinella to wait for Eddie and me. It seemed like a week had gone by since that time.

A week of worry and fear.

A week of indecision.

Suddenly, I didn't think I could face the viewing again. I closed my eyes and rested my head back against the wall.

My thoughts roiled. A whirlwind of conflicting emotions sat just under the surface, ready to burst free at the slightest provocation.

I suddenly missed my safe, cozy little apartment with a deep, painful ache.

The sound of wheels on carpet had me opening my eyes and I focused on a woman wearing an apron and a white paper cap over her hair, heading toward the lecture hall.

Someone had ordered coffee for the room.

I leaned my head back again and sighed, realizing I could use some coffee. After another moment, I forced myself to stand and started toward the room. The sooner we finished the viewing, the sooner I could leave. In that moment, I realized I'd already given up on finding our killer.

Heading toward the lecture room and the mock viewing, I was so lost in my thoughts, I nearly missed the splotches of something red on the carpet. I jolted to a stop, eyeing the substance for a moment before realizing that the reddish streaks on the rug weren't random design points. A closer inspection led me to think they were meant to portray blood. Though, unless I was really off base, I thought the substance was something else entirely.

The marks led away from the lobby, down another hall where I hadn't spent much time. The wide hallway was dark and quiet in the late afternoon, with only the long windows around a distant doorway to soften the shadows.

Instinctively realizing what the marks on the carpet meant. I pulled out my cell and called Eddie. He didn't answer so I left him a quick voicemail and decided to follow the trail myself to see where it led.

Even as I let my curiosity get the best of me, I knew it was a mistake. One that might easily prove fatal.

The smeared lines on the carpet led past the restrooms

and a series of doors marked additional lecture rooms. The trail stopped near a glass-encased garden room, which was currently being watered by an overhead system that mimicked rain.

The end of the trail was marked by a large, moist spot of "blood" where the substance I'd been following had seeped into the rug, as if someone had dropped a bleeding body to do something...

I glanced around, my eyes widening.

"Something like opening a door," I murmured, eyeing a bloody hand print that had been partially washed away by the watering system inside the garden room. I cautiously moved closer to the glass wall, seeing nothing except a tidy stone walkway that wound through the big room filled with flowers and greenery.

My cell rang as I opened the door and peered inside.

I ignored it.

"Hello?" I called out, feeling silly for yelling into the seemingly empty space. But someone had taken pains to create a trail to that spot. And I was just curious enough to want to know why. "Is anybody in here?"

As my tension rose, my ringing phone seemed to grow more insistent.

The more deeply I went into the moist, and muggy room, the ringing seemed muted by the abundance of green and growing things.

I followed the stone path, my gaze sliding constantly over the room. The hairs on my arms lifted as I moved through the too-quiet space. If someone had asked, I wouldn't have been able to describe what I was feeling. The room appeared empty except for the plants. But something told me it wasn't. The air was alive with expectation, causing my skin to itch with the feeling that I was being watched.

The phone finally stopped ringing, only to start up again almost immediately.

Thankfully the "rain" had stopped when I opened the door and I wondered if it was on some kind of motion sensor so hotel guests could walk through the space without fear of getting watered. "Is anybody here?"

My question was met with the sound of water dripping off leaves.

I was halfway through the verdant space when I decided I couldn't take the ringing anymore.

I hit the Answer button just as something snaked out of a rhododendron bush and wrapped around my ankle like a vise, yanking hard.

My blood-curdling scream was the only thing Deitz heard as I answered his call.

12

"**M**ay!" His voice was frantic, the altered cadence telling me he'd taken off running. "Where?"

"Garden room," I responded breathlessly. "Hurry!"

I dropped the phone and tried to yank my leg away from the bloody claws encircling it. But the claws felt like iron bands around my flesh, and they seemed to be getting tighter by the moment.

In a move bred of desperation, I kicked out instead of yanking away, and earned myself a slight reprieve. The grip loosened. I yanked again, only to have my leg ripped out from under me with breathless ease.

I screamed as I toppled backward, falling into a flowering bush that could as easily have been a large porcupine for all the painful holes it put into my flesh.

The sweet smell of roses found its way past my panic too late. I'd already reached for a branch to stop myself from hitting the ground and felt the painful sting of copious thorns in my palm.

The bush in front of me gave a violent shake and a nightmare eased through its shiny leaves.

A bloody visage looked up at me, a plea in its eyes. The whites of those eyes were shocking against a background of glossy red blood.

"Please," the specter ground out in a painful wheeze. "Help..." And then the man's grip on my ankle eased and his head fell to the rich black dirt. Jessie Marks didn't move after that, his big form as still as death.

The garden room door crashed open. "May?!"

"Over here," I called out, falling to my knees even as my heart beat a dangerous rhythm against my ribs. "Jessie Marks has been attacked."

He rounded a curve in the walkway at full speed and screeched to a halt in front of me. His hands found my shoulders as his gaze slipped quickly over me. "Are you okay? Why did you scream? You scared a poop emoji out of me."

His statement had the desired effect and I laughed, the sound slightly hysterical. The door smacked open again and Argh's deep voice ripped the grim smile off my face. "MayBell?!"

"Here," I called out. "It's Jessie Marks."

Argh's judgy gaze skimmed me quickly and then fell to Jessie. Two worry lines found the smooth skin between his eyes. "Is he dead?"

"I'm not sure. He wasn't a minute ago." My gaze fell to my bloody ankle, which still throbbed from his relentless grip.

"You're bleeding," Argh said, his gray gaze hardening accusingly on me.

I rolled my eyes. "You can't blame me for that, superpatch. It's not my blood. Jessie was trying to get my attention."

"Ah," Eddie said. "Thus the scream."

"Yep."

"Sorry I didn't get your call right away," Deitz said. "Remember that number we found in the vict..."

I nudged him with my elbow and he looked at Argh, whose expression had turned hostile. "The victim's what?" my brother asked. "Please tell me you didn't go into her room? It hasn't been fully processed yet."

Eddie laughed. "Don't be stupid. We'd never do that."

"Uh, huh," Argh said, clearly not believing Deitz.

My PI turned back to me. "Anyway, you know that piece of paper you found on the floor with the number?"

I nodded, studiously avoiding Argh's glare.

"They called me back. It was a dry cleaner. They didn't even know An...um...the client."

Argh swore softly. "You two are going to be the death of me."

"Detective Ferth?" a female voice called from the door. I could tell by the top of the glossy blonde head I could see above the vegetation, that it was likely Officer Sarah.

"Call an ambulance," Argh barked. He bent over Marks to feel for a pulse.

Officer Sarah's head bobbed in the affirmative and she disappeared back out the door.

"Is he?" I asked, using the sibling shorthand Argh and I had perfected over the years.

Argh straightened, wiping his hands over his jeans and depositing a healthy swatch of blood there. "His pulse is weak and he seems to have lost a lot of blood."

I frowned. "But..."

"Thanks to you finding him, he'll probably make it."

The tightness in my chest eased a bit. "Stabbed?"

Argh grimaced. "More like sawed on. It's got to be our killer." The words seemed to snap him out of his thoughts and he refocused on me with a judgy gray gaze. "Which begs the question, why are you here instead of trying to entice the killer out of hiding?"

I didn't let his attitude get to me. I knew my brother better than he knew himself. He tended to blame me irrationally for stuff when he was worried about me. "I'm fine, Argh."

His frown only deepened. He turned to Deitz. "And you? Why'd you leave your post?"

Eddie stared at him for a beat and then said, "Well, duh."

Argh flushed. Obviously Eddie would come to me if he thought I was in danger. "The more important question," I said, "Is why are *you* here? I thought you'd left the hotel."

Argh stared at Jessie Marks, his expression grim. "I'm back. Your boyfriend notified me that you'd sent a 9-1-1." He glowered at me. "It's a good thing too, since my own sister didn't bother to tell me when she was in trouble."

I expelled air in frustration. "I was a little busy following the blood trail to the nearly dead man in the rose bushes."

Argh just shook his head.

Unfortunately, I realized, with all of us away, the killer was free to do what killers did. "We need to get back to the room," I said. Doug and Pinella were there and dozens of other people who wouldn't have a clue they were in danger until it was too late.

"Yes, you do," Argh agreed. Sirens flared through the quiet normalcy of the outside world and his gaze slid toward the sound. "But first you need to tell me what's going on here."

As quickly as possible, I told him about speaking to the women in the ladies' room, walking out to find the faux bloody trail, and then following it to find Marks.

"I think it was fake blood," I told them. "It's a theater prop. The stuff comes in a tube and it's in gel form."

"Why would someone create a fake blood trail," Argh asked, looking dubious.

"For someone to follow?" I asked, shrugging. "Whoever attacked Marks wanted him found."

"The trail started by the restrooms?" Eddie asked.

"Near there, yes. It was probably meant to appear that Jessie had been heading to the men's room when he was attacked."

"And nobody saw anything?" Argh asked, his voice incredulous.

"That's not too surprising," Eddie said. "With the shooting and murder, the hotel has gone to minimal coverage to protect its employees. There were very few non-convention guests and most of them have been staying in their rooms until the police give them the go-ahead to leave. The spot May described is also out of sight of the front desk. Since the convention attendees were mostly ensconced in the big room, there weren't many people around to see it."

I thought of the two women. "You might want to try to find those women I spoke to," I told Argh. "They left the ladies' room before I did. Maybe they saw something."

Argh made an exaggerated motion of relief. "Thank goodness you're here to tell me how to do my job, Maybenot. Otherwise, I might have walked across the street and interviewed the wrong people. What would I do without you? Thank you so much."

I grinned. "You're welcome, superpatch."

He sighed. "Get out of here, you two. Keep to the original

plan. The only thing this tells us is that Marks probably isn't our killer."

JOSHUA BARNFORD MET us half-way across the lobby, his attractive face creased with worry. "Who was killed this time?" It seemed as if he kept his voice low with an effort. He was clearly upset. "We should cancel the convention and send everybody home." Running long fingers through his sandy hair, he seemed jittery and off balance. It was a look that didn't sit well on him. Barnford struck me as someone who was always in control.

"A man was attacked," Eddie said. "As far as we know he's still alive."

"Who was it?" Barnford barked the question as if he was used to being obeyed when he spoke.

Though Deitz stiffened slightly, he gave Barnford a grim smile. "You'll need to speak to the detective in charge about that."

Eddie gently clasped my elbow, steering me around the event organizer.

Barnford followed us toward the door, his long strides easily keeping up. "Where *is* Ferth? Why isn't he here?"

"He's here," I said, feeling the need to defend my brother. Which was odd because Argh would be the first to argue he didn't need my help. "He's with the b...victim."

"You were going to say *body*, weren't you?" Barnford said, slamming a hand on the door when Deitz reached for it. "We need to get everyone out of here."

Eddie leaned close to the other man, no smile in evidence as he spoke slowly and firmly. "You need to speak to Detective Ferth. We have no control over anything except ourselves. I believe I speak for both Ms. Ferth and myself when I say we're not going anywhere until the killer is found. Now, please move out of our way or I'll move you myself."

Barnford paled, but inclined his head. "Of course. I apologize. I've never had anything like this happen at one of my events. I'm afraid it's thrown me a bit."

"And hopefully you never will again," Eddie responded before yanking the door open and urging me inside with a gentle hand on my back. "But we all need to remain calm, Mr. Barnford. Especially those who people look to for guidance in this difficult situation."

Barnford closed his eyes for a beat and then opened them, nodding. "Understood."

We entered the room and discovered that the funereal atmosphere had evaporated. People sat in clusters, drinking coffee and something else in plastic cups. From the jovial mood, I thought the "something else" might be 100 proof.

But worse than that, the corpse was holding court across the room and her grieving nephew was yukking it up with the rest of them.

Eddie and I exchanged a look and started toward the casket brigade. I glared at the group in the folding chairs on our way by and they snapped to, several of them standing and pasting sad expressions on their faces.

"What a cluster-cluck," I murmured, earning myself a soft chuckle from Deitz.

Doug turned as we approached, his boyish face brightening when he saw us. "Here they are! We thought you guys got lost."

The group turned as one, every face bearing a sloppy smile and a lidded gaze. The strong smell of alcohol stung my nostrils as we approached. I glared at Doug. His smile drooped slightly.

"Hey, dolly!" Pinella was draped over the side of the coffin, her chin resting on the satin padding, staining it with her bright red lipstick. "Why so glum?"

I ignored her, focusing on Doug. "Have you been drinking?"

His slightly blurry gaze widened with affront. "Dude!"

I grabbed the plastic cup in his hand and sniffed. It reeked of alcohol. "I can't believe you are all drinking. How unprofessional can you be?"

Though faces all around me fell, I heard giggling coming from somewhere to the side of the room. As I watched, the heavy drapes the hotel used to separate rooms rippled and bulged outward. A trim backside broke through, wriggled seductively, and then yanked the rest of a petite blonde into the room. The woman I'd spoken to in the restroom earlier stumbled backward, shrieking with hilarity and then gasping as the contents of her punch splashed dangerously close to her cream-colored blouse.

Without delay, the drapes rippled again and a tall figure emerged, his too-handsome face split in a wide grin. He too held a cup of punch. But, unlike his friend, he didn't seem nearly so affected by it. Seeing me, Peter Steel lifted his hand in salute and the blonde woman from the ladies' room started giggling again.

"Who spiked the punch?" Eddie called out for the room to hear.

Conversation sliced off at his question, and several wobbly mourners squinted down at their cups as if they'd just discovered they were holding them.

One of the hotel staff brought in a cart with punch,"

Doug said, frowning at the contents of his cup. We thought you'd approved it."

"I did not approve spiked punch," I said primly.

"It's okay," the corpse said, followed by a loud hiccup. "We're just havin' a little fun, dolly."

"This isn't the time for fun," I said, sounding way too much like the Lieutenant for my comfort. "This is a job. A viewing. You're all professionals. Act like it!"

Grumbling acquiescence had them all straightening their spines and reluctantly abandoning their cups. I glanced at Eddie. "Can you find someone to bring us coffee? Lots of it?"

He nodded and I set about trying to pull my fake viewing back into line. I turned to the corpse. "Time for you to take a nap, Angeline."

At the firm tone of my voice, she winked and fell backward into the casket, her cup of punch hitting the floor at the base of the stand. Several people yelped as the red liquid splashed their slacks and legs.

"Back to positions, people. The siblings are back on point to accept condolences in one..." I glared around. "Two..." People started to move. "Three!"

Doug and I were suddenly standing alone. I caught his eye and he grimaced. "Dude!"

Shrugging, I said, "It had to be done."

Doug opened his mouth but I stopped him with a raised pointer finger. "Don't even say I sounded like the Lieutenant."

His lips slammed shut, leaving me with that uncomfortable feeling you get when you're over thirty and you can hear your parents in your own voice. "It couldn't be helped."

"If you say so," Doug muttered.

An older woman, her unlined, attractive face formed

into a politely sad expression, approached us with one hand extended. "Polly Pearson," she said, her lips twitching on the name. "I'm so sorry about your Aunt Angeline. She was a wonderful woman and a wizard with a whip."

Giggles sounded all around us and I glared at the woman in front of us. "Very funny. Go..." I shooed her away with a flap of my hand. "Tell the corpse to stop snoring."

"Dude." Doug said in a disapproving tone. "Don't disturb the dead."

I sighed. "I'm in alliteration Hades."

Peter Steel approached, his smile not at all sad. "Nice party." He winked at me. "If I'd known poor Angeline had such a lovely niece, I'd have begged her for an introduction long ago."

"Dude," Doug said, disapproving again.

Steel chuckled. "Sorry. I'll get back to work schooling the mourners."

"You do that," I said. "They need it."

He nodded happily.

A slender man with a thick mop of graying brown hair took Doug's hand. "I'm so sorry for your loss."

Doug nodded. "Dude."

The man turned to me. "Your aunt was the kindest woman I've ever met."

I clasped his hand. "How did you meet Angeline?" I tried to remember the basics of the script I'd skimmed with all the background information for mourners and faux family to use.

"At a charity dinner in support of an animal rescue organization. She spoke eloquently about the need to rescue rather than adopt. I'll admit she won a bit of my heart with that speech."

I nodded and Doug said, "Dude," clearly touched.

The man's face folded into a mask of grief. "I have to ask...how did she die?"

I thought of my mother and a tear popped out of my eye right on cue. My lips quivering, I sniffled daintily, holding a tissue to my nose. "The police are trying to keep it quiet, but she was murdered."

An expression of horror left his lips and he stumbled back a step. "Murder?"

I motioned for him to lower his voice. "The police are trying to keep it quiet."

Nodding, he leaned in, his voice low. "How?"

I shook my head, tears flowing freely down my cheek as I held the eau de onion slathered tissue near my eyes. The concoction on the tissue didn't smell like onion but apparently included a good dose of whatever caused tearing up. I intended to pick up several more bottles of the stuff the following day, when the industry vendors arrived to show off the innovations and improvements from the previous year.

I sniffed, dabbing my nose. "The police said she was strangled."

The man frowned. "Strangled? But wasn't there blood?"

I gave a quiet sob. "Yes. She was strangled and then her throat was cut. It's all so horrifying."

The man clucked his tongue in sympathy. "How terrible for you."

I nodded. "But, fortunately, they were able to pull a latent print from her throat. They think they know who killed her."

The man glanced around. "Have they arrested him yet?"

"It's only a matter of time," Doug said in a "dun, dun, dun" voice.

A line had formed behind the man as we spoke to him.

As he stepped away, a short, balding man with a chin a turkey would envy stepped up and we all recited our lines, which reflected a version of the same script.

Everyone wanted to know how Angeline died.

Everyone showed their shock when we told them she'd been murdered.

Everyone was relieved to hear the police had a suspect.

And every time I went through the script, I couldn't help wondering if I was talking directly to the killer.

13

After two hours of playing his part, Doug proclaimed the need to visit the men's room and I was exhausted. I dropped into a chair and listened to the rumbling snores of our corpse. Kicking off my shoes, I worked my toes against the carpet and groaned with relief.

A steaming mug of coffee appeared in front of my face. I took it as Argh dropped wearily into a chair next to me. "How's Marks?" I asked, holding the heated mug between icy fingers.

"He'll be okay. The cuts on his throat were hesitation cuts. It looks like the attacker chickened out and tried to strangle him instead."

"Isn't that strange?" I asked Argh. It wasn't often I found him in a talkative mood when it came to an investigation. Usually, he told me to mind my own business.

He nodded. "The hesitation cut indicates someone who isn't confident or who doesn't like killing with a blade."

"Like a woman?" I offered. I sipped the coffee he'd

brought me and nearly moaned with pleasure as it forged a warm path down my throat.

"It's possible, I guess. But it would be a rare woman who had strong enough hands to strangle a man."

"If she used a choke hold..."

He stopped me with a shake of his head. "There are finger bruises on the skin."

I frowned thoughtfully. "Two killers?"

Argh expelled a long breath. "It's one of our working theories. But I don't like it."

We sat in silence for a long moment, thinking.

I had a crazy thought. One I wasn't sure enough about to voice. But when my brother didn't come up with anything of his own, I decided to offer it up. "Do you find it strange that Marks was attacked in a way that mimics our misinformation campaign?"

Argh looked at me and frowned. "I'm listening."

I went on, hoping to clarify. "We tried to convince the killer you had a fingerprint that would point a finger at him. We hoped that would bring him out into the open, force him to take the offense. But what if the killer is so arrogant he decided to show us what it would look like if he did as we'd accused?"

"A warning?" Argh asked.

I shrugged. "Maybe."

Argh's frown deepened. Finally, he expelled a sigh. "It's crazy, but I'll agree the coincidence is too much. If Marks had died, it would have been in exactly the way we suggested."

I thought of the spiked punch. "I don't think serving spiked punch at our faux viewing was a mistake either. This guy's cocky. He's proving he can control any situation we give him."

Argh nodded. "I spoke to the kitchen. They insist they got a call from someone who was with the convention asking for the punch."

"I'm guessing Marks didn't see his attacker?" I asked.

"No. He heard a foot scuff and smelled something fruity. But as he turned, the knife flashed and he remembered a burning pain. He managed to hit the attacker with an elbow to the ribs...thinks the guy might have a cracked rib. That could come in useful."

I nodded. "I'll watch for anybody favoring their sides or walking as if in pain."

Argh and I sat in companionable silence for several minutes, our gazes sliding around the room looking for tell-tale winces or protective maneuvers. Nobody appeared to be in pain. Of course, with the amount of punch some of them had imbibed, they'd be feeling no pain for a while.

"Any noticeable reactions to the information you've been spreading?"

"Not really. Micro-expressions maybe. But nothing you could turn into a charge."

He looked at me in surprise and I fought a smug smile, silently thanking Peter Steel for his lecture segment on micro-expressions. Finally, Argh nodded, shoving wearily to his feet. "You can close it down, I guess. We've done all we can here."

"But what about finding the killer?"

"We'll give him some time to process the information about the fingerprint. He'll come to the obvious conclusion and hopefully make a mistake."

I frowned, thinking the profile of the killer I'd been building didn't support my brother's hopes. "You'll have to let Barnford shut down the convention. He's already making noises about it."

"I plan on it. We have everyone's information. Those who've come from out of town have been instructed not to leave. It's the best we can do."

"When you talked to Angeline's family, did you ask about a husband? Boyfriend?"

He gave me a look and I held up my hands in apology. "I just wondered if she had someone who cared about her." Tears burned my eyes at the thought that she might not.

"No spouse that we can determine. One brother and one living parent. Her mother. Apparently, they weren't close. I mostly worked with the brother to create the viewing scenario."

Sadness made my chest tight. I hadn't spoken directly to the victim, had only seen her after death, but somehow I felt as if we could have been friends. I felt as if I knew her in a way I didn't know many people. I'd experienced her best and worst traits. I knew she'd loved animals and enjoyed making people laugh. I also knew she tended to push people away. I suspected she'd been sometimes lonely and habitually alone. That knowledge made me appreciate the family I had. They were often annoying. They inserted themselves regularly into my life. But they did it for all the best reasons. They loved me, and each and every one of them would put their lives on the line...had done it more than once...to keep me safe.

I leaned my head against my brother's shoulder and we had a moment of uncharacteristic bonding.

When he stood a few minutes later, Argh patted my shoulder and gifted me with his trademark glower. "Be careful."

I drooped in my chair for several minutes after he left, feeling defeated. I hated to think a killer was going to just walk out of the hotel because we weren't good enough to catch him.

"Hey, dolly," Pinella said, dropping into the chair my brother had just vacated. "Why so glum?"

I shrugged. "I thought we'd get him." Laughing bitterly at myself, I swiped tears off my cheeks. "Stupid me. I thought our little ruse would drag the killer from the shadows."

She patted my knee. "It still might, dolly. He's not going to jump up and down and declare himself the killer. His first thought will likely be to escape the hotel."

I nodded, knowing she was right. I hoped Argh's coverage was good enough to hold him. Then I realized it didn't matter. Argh was going to have to let everybody go.

"He'll want to tie up loose ends. Look for leverage," Pinella said with the confidence of someone who watched *all* the cop and forensics shows.

My mind roiled with potential problems and I almost didn't hear what Pinella said. Then it hit my psyche like a flash flood, raging through me. My head snapped around and I fixed her with a stunned look.

Escape. Leverage. I knew she was right. Suddenly, I was on my feet and running. The killer would need leverage to get out of the hotel. And I was pretty sure I knew what leverage he'd try to use.

"May?" Eddie called as I whipped past Doug and him standing near the door.

I didn't stop, didn't slow. Horror had me whipped into a mindless state.

"Dude?" said a breathy voice at my elbow a few seconds later.

I turned to find Doug keeping up with me as I headed for the elevator. "Shakes is in danger," I told him, and it was enough. He picked up speed, reaching the elevator and slamming a palm over the "Up" button.

We stood panting as the elevator groaned and dithered and generally took its time coming to us. My nerves wouldn't allow me to wait. "Jeezopete!" I turned and ran for the stairs, not bothering to look back to see if Doug was with me.

He was. I heard him pounding along behind me as we flew up one short rise of stairs after another until we hit the one marked with a five.

Doug was breathing heavily, but still running when we hit the hallway and started toward my room about midway down. My ears strained for the sound of my little dog yipping.

I didn't hear anything. In fact, the entire floor was too quiet. No voices softened the terror in my chest. No hair dryers thrummed behind closed doors. No footsteps sounded. No doors slammed.

It was as if Doug and I were entirely alone in the big hotel.

Ice crawled down my spine as I fumbled for my room key, my fingers mishandling and dropping it twice before Doug took it away and used it to open my door. He placed a hand on my arm, trying to stop me from barreling through it in search of my dog, but I shook him off. "Shakes!"

I knew as soon as I entered the room that he wasn't there. But someone else had been. I frantically searched the main room. Looked under the beds. Doug ducked right and went into the bathroom. I yanked open the closet door, hoping against hope my sweet dog would be cowering there. Scared but safe.

No Shakespeare crouched among the copious numbers

of shoes stuffed into the small closet. Doug's voice came to me, filled with dread. "May. You need to come in here."

Everything in me rebelled at the idea. Every cell in my body shrank away from what I might see if I did as he said. But I had to know.

I had to see.

I really didn't want to see.

I forced one foot in front of the other and stepped through the open bathroom door. Doug stood in front of the sink, his face pale and murder in his brown eyes.

I followed the line of his sight and my knees buckled. Gasping in fear, I would have hit the floor if Doug hadn't moved fast.

"He'll die." Two short words, scrawled across the mirror in front of us. The killer had used my own lipstick to send me the terrifying message.

My head was shaking. My heart pounding so hard I thought I might pass out. "No," I whispered, the single word infused with a prayer.

"What does it mean?" Doug asked, his voice soft.

Anger flared. Anger at Doug for asking me a stupid question. Anger at the killer for taking my dog. Anger at myself for not keeping Shakes close.

My phone rang. In full-on panic, I stabbed the button to answer it, hope soaring. Maybe Shakes got away. Maybe the note on my mirror was just a mean-tempered prank. Maybe he was okay.

"Hello!?"

"He'll die." It was a harsh, unrecognizable whisper.

My legs gave way and all Doug could do was keep me from hitting the floor too hard. "What do you want?"

"You'll get me out of here."

"That won't be..."

"Stop talking or he'll die."

My lips slammed shut. The unfairness of everything hit me hard enough to stop air from reaching my lungs. I fought to breathe, unable to speak for the struggle. Doug gently pushed my head down between my knees and crouched beside me, rubbing my back.

"Meet me near the lobby stairs in five minutes. Leave your phone behind. If you bring anyone else or try to interfere in any way with my escape, he'll die. Do you understand?"

I nodded because it was all I could do.

"Do. You. Understand?" the voice ground out, enraged at my non-response.

"Yes," I wheezed. I fought to calm down, knowing if I passed out or lost it, my dog would suffer. "I'll be there."

The call disconnected. I looked at Doug. Tears were a heavy stream down my face.

He clasped my icy hands and made me look into his eyes. "You can do this. You're an actor. You can act strong, even if you're not feeling it. Right?"

I pulled in a deep breath, held it for a beat, and then let it go, nodding. "Yes."

"I'll find Argh. We'll head you off. When the killer's distracted, you grab Shakes."

It was a silly plan. Inadequate and unlikely to work, but it was something for me to cling to. I nodded.

Doug helped me to my feet and I splashed cold water over my face, shoving hair out of my eyes and staring at the mirror. I wanted to wipe the horrible message off the glass in the worst way. But it was evidence. Argh would need to see it. I turned away from it, gave Doug a hug. "Be careful," we both said at once.

His smile was his usual slightly goofy one. "Jinx."

"Jinx yourself," I said on a watery chuckle. Rubbing my hands on my jeans, I took another deep breath and headed toward the door. "Stay in the room for a few beats, just in case he's watching. Call Argh as soon as you know I'm in the stairwell. Take the elevator," I instructed. I didn't want the killer to see Doug and realize he'd been in the room when he'd called. The last thing I needed was for my friend to suffer too.

"Dude..." he said, giving me a look.

"Wish me luck," I said.

"Luck," he responded.

And then I was alone in the hallway, all but running for the stairs.

14

I burst through the lobby door and stopped, looking around for my dog. I didn't see him, and I didn't see anyone who looked as if they were looking for me. I moved away from the doors so I could see into the lobby. Long lines had formed at the checkout counter and uniformed police were questioning each person trying to check out, jotting down their personal and contact information before allowing them to leave.

Police blocked the front door too. It was likely they were stationed at all other exits and in the parking garage below. I wondered how the killer expected me to get him out. The police were going to stop me as quickly as they'd stop someone else.

Unless Argh got involved.

I closed my eyes, realizing I should have given more thought to my rescue operation. By flying downstairs to save my dog, I'd made myself as much of a potential victim as Shakes was. When I opened them again, my gaze landed on Officer Sarah, whose expression when she saw me turned sour.

I started forward, intending to ask the uniformed cop where my brother was. The question never left my lips. I spotted the next wave of trouble the moment Sarah did and jerked to a stop on a strangled gasp.

A man stood in front of the elevators with a gun in his hand. The lovely Sarah wasted no time grabbing her weapon and training it on the newcomer. "Drop the gun, sir," she said as screams erupted through the lobby and people ran for cover wherever they could find it.

The man's face was a mask of rage, his smallish eyes aflame with the same emotion. "He killed her. I'll give you my gun as soon as Steel and I have finished our business."

All eyes skimmed to the tall man standing in the center of the lobby, arms up and hands flat as if to ward off the bullet with his name on it. Peter Steel shook his head, his gaze wide. "I...I don't know who you are..."

"My name doesn't matter!" the man screamed. Several people screamed and crouched closer to the ground as the gun swung wildly with his movement. "Her name was Angeline. She was a bright star in my life. She was going to be my wife. And you killed her. You lied to her. Manipulated her. And then you killed her when she refused to do as you asked."

Steel's expression hardened. His body turned to iron as he shook his head again. "No. I'd never hurt Angel..."

"Don't!" the man screamed. "Never say her name with your foul, lying mouth."

Steel lifted his hands higher, nodding. "Okay. I won't say her name. But I promise you I had nothing to do with her death. I lo..." He swallowed hard, seemingly rethinking what he'd been about to say. "I cared for her. We were friends. Just friends."

The man by the elevators shook his head hard. The gun bobbled in his hand and he nearly dropped it.

Sarah took two quick steps before the man saw her and lifted the gun toward Steel again. "Come any closer and I'll shoot him."

Sarah held her ground, her gaze skimming quickly to the desk and then away.

A dark head moved just below the surface of the counter. A familiar dark head. I wanted to swear. But the man with the gun didn't notice.

"You offered her a job so you could control her. You promised her things you could never deliver. But Angie wasn't as stupid as you thought. She knew what you were doing. She would never have taken you up on that job. She and I were going to get married. She loved me."

The last three words were flavored with a level of desperation that told me he didn't really believe them. He was striking out in his grief, but somewhere deep down he knew Angeline hadn't been the woman she'd pretended to be.

"I'm sure she loved you," Steel said, clearly picking up on the same note of desperation I had. "She mentioned you to me. She said she was going to marry you. I promise. We were just friends. We talked as friends did. Nothing more."

The man's expression softened, and tears wet his cheeks. He succumbed to sobbing, and his shoulders drooped. The hand holding the gun slid downward several inches, until it was no longer pointed at Steel. I allowed myself to breathe as it appeared the man would give up his gun.

Sarah slowly extended a hand. "Sir, why don't you give me the gun? You don't want to hurt anybody, do you?"

He appeared to be softening. He started to turn, but the

elevator dinged and his body stiffened again. He swung toward the sound, the gun suddenly pointed right at me.

The elevator door opened behind me, and Doug came flying out, eyes wild. "Dude!"

Several things happened after that. The world passed by in slow motion as the man's knuckles turned white and his finger compressed the trigger.

"Down!" I screamed, diving on Doug and taking him to the ground with me.

Eddie yelled my name.

Argh bellowed at the shooter.

The bullet slammed into metal somewhere behind me. I couldn't look up as gunshots flared all around us and people screamed.

The world was a chaos of sound and motion and the space between my shoulder blades prickled as I imagined the gun being swung our way.

A man yelped in pain and then howled as panic gave way to real agony.

Below me Doug grunted. "Dude, you need to stop eating so much. You're heavy."

"Stay down and still," I said in a harsh whisper. "He's got a gun."

"Well, duh," came the irreverent response beneath my draping arm.

When the screaming finally stopped, I risked a look up and saw Argh with a knee on the man's back, slapping cuffs onto his hands behind his back. When the gunman was safely cuffed, Argh tugged him off the ground.

Next to Argh, the man looked small, his head barely reaching Argh's chin and his features almost too delicate to be a man's.

I rolled to my feet and reached down to help Doug rise.

A large pair of feet appeared in my view and hands caught me beneath the arms to help me rise. Peter Steel gave me a look I couldn't identify. "Are you both okay?"

I nodded. "You?"

"Better than I should be," he said, wincing. "I swear, I didn't know she had a fiancé."

I stared at him for a long moment. Then, acting on instinct, I asked. "Did you kill her?"

Steel seemed to choke, his words getting caught in his throat. Finally, he shook his head and turned away. I wasn't sure if he was denying the possibility, or just disgusted that I'd asked.

"May?" Eddie grabbed me up and yanked me into a hug that compressed my lungs. "You're okay? I just about lost my mind when the gun swung your way." His hug tightened and I squeaked. "Argh is right, you're a trouble magnet. You attract it like honey draws a bear."

My gaze slid toward the door and I found Argh looking at me, his expression forming a question his worried gaze couldn't hide.

I nodded and he gave me a smile, turning away to haul his prisoner out of the hotel.

"What are the chances that man killed Angeline himself?" I asked Deitz as he finally released me.

"Pretty good, I'd say."

"Dude?" Doug reached out to clasp my hand.

"I'm okay," I said, patting his chest.

"Where's Shakes?" Eddie asked, and my heart tightened painfully. I'd had an assignation I'd failed to make. Would my dog suffer for my mistake?

Pinella appeared from the midst of the crowd, her pale, wrinkled face filled with terror. "Dolly! I'm sorry. I didn't know what he was going to do."

"What's wrong?" I asked, grabbing her as she barreled into me.

Her hand lifted to her throat in an unconscious gesture of distress. She scanned a worried gaze toward the door. "He threatened me. He said he'd kill you."

The message on the mirror! Was Pinella the person I was supposed to meet near the elevators?

"Was it that man out there?" I asked her. "Did he tell you to approach me?"

Her lips quivered and her fingers tensed against her throat. "I don't know who. He..." She swallowed hard, wincing. "I didn't see him. He grabbed me in the big room and told me he'd kill you if you didn't do as he said. He said I could save your life or kill you."

As tears spilled over her cheeks, I pulled her into a hug. "You aren't responsible for my living or dying." But, when I pulled back, I saw the half-inch line of blood on her thin-skinned, wrinkled throat. I grabbed the fingers she quickly used to cover the wound. "He cut you?!" The words came out in a growl that made Pinella blink.

"I didn't want to involve you," she explained. "I didn't want him to hurt you."

I hugged her again, holding her more tightly than I should. Pinella pushed on me for release.

"Where's the little furry dude?"

Alarm clutched my chest with icy claws. Not responding to Doug, I swung to Eddie. "The killer has Shakes. He's holding him as leverage to get me."

"Why you?" Eddie asked.

"He wants to use me to get out of here."

We all looked toward the police car still at the curb. Angeline's fiancé huddled miserably in the back seat.

I took off, shoving the door open. A lowering sun bathed

me in warmth, the horizon painted in pinks, purples and golds as day eased toward night. I barely noticed the stunning beauty as I reached for the handle to open the car door. Argh's hand covered mine, stopping me. "What are you doing, May?"

"Do you know if that man was a guest at the hotel?"

Argh frowned. "I'm not sure. I don't think so."

My shoulders sagged. But I knew I couldn't let him leave without at least asking. "I need to question your prisoner about Shakes."

Argh frowned. "Shakes? What about him?"

"The killer took him." Tears burned tracks down my cheeks. "I have to find out where he is."

Argh stared at me for a long moment, emotions flitting visibly through his intense gray gaze. Then he nodded. "Stay back. I'll ask him."

Wrapping my arms around myself, I reluctantly did as my brother requested. But I felt as if I was going to jump right out of my skin if he didn't get the answers I needed, and fast.

"Mr. Smith," Argh said to the man inside the cruiser. "Did you take a small gray dog from that woman over there?"

Smith, because that was apparently his name, glared over at me, something cold swimming through his light-colored eyes. "I've never seen her before in my life."

I made a small sound of pain and Eddie wrapped an arm around my waist, holding me in place.

"She believes you kidnapped her dog so she'd help you get out of the hotel."

The man gave a bitter laugh. "I've been scoping the hotel out for days. I know every inch of that place. If I'd wanted to escape, I'd have just used the door in the boiler room. But I didn't want to escape. I wanted to kill the man who killed my Angie."

My gaze flew to Eddie's and I turned on my heel, running before I gave any thought to what I was doing. Argh called after me, but Deitz apparently knew it would be a waste of time trying to talk me out of it. He just fell into step alongside me.

I ran to the counter and caught the attention of the first clerk. "Boiler room?"

She frowned. "That's not a public space..."

Deitz whipped out his credentials and flashed them at her too quickly for her to realize they weren't a badge. "Police business," he said.

She chewed the inside of her lip for a beat and then nodded, pulling a key card from her pocket. "Don't lose this. Bring it back to me when you're done."

I nodded, snatching the card out of her hand. "How do we get there?"

"Basement level. It's the door across from the pool."

We didn't bother waiting for the elevator. We took the stairs at a full-out run and shoved the door open without stopping. The heavy door slammed into the wall behind it and the sound ricocheted down the concrete-walled hall as we followed the scent of chlorine to our destination. The pool was empty and silent, no families enjoying its warm, wet embrace. The silence fit my mood, reinforcing the surreal quality of the last couple of days.

A moment later we saw the door we needed...plain metal, painted an industrial gray with a sign that read, Employees Only.

I fumbled so badly with the key card Eddie took it from me and slipped it through the reader. The lock snicked and a green light told us it was unlocked.

We shared a quick look and plunged into the dimly-lit room. Eddie flipped the switch next to the door and nothing happened for a beat, then the row of fluorescent lights running down the center of the long room buzzed and flickered on.

The door clicked shut after a delay of a couple of seconds, cutting us off from the rest of the world.

The place looked like an alien spaceship. It was filled with a mutant army of metal and plastic equipment with coiled limbs that made passage through the room difficult. Water trickled from something in the back corner, the sound somehow rising above the constant drone that filled the space, along with the occasional clicks and whirs of things I wouldn't be able to identify if I were standing right next to them. More than once, I wished I had a flashlight to peer into the crevices between the various types of equipment.

"Shakes?" I called out, praying my little guy would be there. I went one way and Eddie went the other, both of us calling for my dog. Despite our persistent calling, Shakes didn't respond to tell us he was there.

Tears blurred the room and I had to stop, fear for my little dog and anguish at the thought I might not get him back brought me to my knees on the hard floor. The single sob that escaped before I could stop it was mercifully drowned out by the drone of the equipment.

Footsteps sounded to my right and light flared over the alien army surrounding me, illuminating their coiled arms and thick metal legs.

A figure slipped silently through a door that, judging by the light touching the equipment above my head, led outside.

I started to rise, but halted in surprise as Eddie's voice rang out in warning. "Hey! Stop!"

That was when I realized I was watching the killer disappear, and possibly my chance to get Shakes back.

I surged to my feet and started to run, my heart pounding hard against my ribs as a new terror replaced the old one. I needed to catch whoever had just left the room, or Shakes might be lost to me forever.

15

A bright overhead light masked the dying sun beyond the door. The brightness of it hit me like a punch to the face as I flew through the door the killer had used. I hesitated for a few seconds, blinking to acclimate to the vivid white light.

"May! Wait."

I didn't slow for Deitz. He was fully capable of catching up, and I thought I'd caught a glimpse of our target rounding a small brick building half a block ahead. The shadows were growing longer by the moment as the sun sank behind the distant trees. Behind the building was a winding, picturesque path that I suspected led to the lake. Behind the lake, in the distance, the jagged outline of mountains rose majestically into the sky.

I took off running, wanting to keep the killer in sight as the shadows swallowed his trail.

With trees and cabin rentals dotting the landscape ahead, I knew it would be all too easy to lose my prey if I didn't keep up.

Behind me, the heavy metal door leading out of the

boiler room slammed closed and Eddie's footsteps pounded over the sidewalk before going quiet as he hit the grass. I stayed close to the tree line so the figure darting through trees and rounding the buildings ahead didn't hear me coming. I hoped Deitz would do the same.

When my prey didn't dart back out from behind a cute gray and white cedar shake cabin, I slowed, leery of the deepening shadows around the cabin that would keep me from seeing if he was waiting to ambush me.

Turning to find Eddie only a few feet away, I motioned toward the cabin and indicated that I wanted to approach from the opposite side. He nodded and veered that way, his sneakers silent in the thick, green grass.

I let him take the lead, my own footfalls sounding like a buffalo navigating a path of dried leaves.

We slowed as we neared the back corner of the little cottage. Pressing close to the side, Eddie slipped past a window and someone screamed. Right behind him, I hit the window just as a woman with tangled wet hair and a towel wrapped around her well-padded form took a deep breath and let loose another scream.

Oops.

On the other side of the building, gravel crunched and a darkly-clad form shot away, leaped over a fire pit, clambered over a small picnic tree, and disappeared into the dense forest of trees that surrounded the hotel.

"Agile," I huffed out as Eddie set a path to follow.

We lost a few seconds bypassing the stuff the runner had leaped and dove into the darkly-threatening woods. Deitz was several long strides ahead of me, so I saw the dark shape of something swing out from behind a large ever-green and catch him across the middle. He went down with a pain-filled grunt and tried to roll away as the object I realized was a branch descended on him again. Judging by the meaty sound of wood slamming into flesh, he didn't roll far enough.

"Eddie!" If I'd been thinking, I'd have gone around the other side of the tree and tackled the runner to the ground. But seeing Eddie under attack made me panic. I ran right for him, gaze focused on the spot where he'd disappeared.

I made myself the perfect target.

The same branch swung my way just as I caught the toe of my shoe in a raised tree root and went down hard enough to knock the wind out of me. As I lay there trying to catch my breath, I was dimly aware of the sound of fleeing footsteps crashing through the darkening woods.

Struggling to breathe, I tried to see Deitz but he'd fallen on the other side of a rotting tree. "Eddie?" I rasped, getting to my hands and knees and crawling toward the last place I'd seen him. "Deitz, talk to me." My voice still sounded slightly strangled, but I was slowly regaining my breath.

He groaned. "I hate the woods."

I tried to chuckle but didn't have enough air in my lungs to do it. "Me too," I wheezed.

"Did he get away?" Eddie asked.

"Yeah." I reached the rotted tree and leaned over it, sucking in air at the sight of a large, gash on Eddie's arm and a bloody knot on his cheek. "Ouch."

"You should see the other guy," he said, sounding breathless.

"I did see him," I said, dropping to my butt and leaning against the tree. "He sprang away from us like a gazelle."

"Hurt me," Deitz complained.

"Too late. The other guy beat me to it." We sat in silence for a few beats, my breaths wheezing loudly into the silence.

Finally, Eddie shoved to his feet with a groan. He stood with one shoulder drooping, holding his arm against his middle.

I stood too. "Is anything broken?" I asked, eyeing him with concern.

"Only my pride."

I held out my hand and he took it. We ambled out of the woods, back toward the path leading to the hotel. We didn't get far. As we stepped out of the trees, a voice called out. "Stop right there. Put your hands in the air."

Eddie tried to lift his arms and hissed in pain. I lifted mine. "What are you doing?" I called out, recognizing the voice.

A man came out from behind the cabin nearest us, gun drawn. He stopped and gaped at Eddie and me, then snapped his mouth closed and holstered his weapon. "I should have known it was you two."

I dropped my arms. "Argh, why were you pointing your gun at us?"

"The hotel got a call from a woman in one of these cabins. Seems she had two peeping Toms." He hesitated, his lips twitching. "Or one peeping Tom and one peeping Tina."

"Har," I said. "We weren't peeping. We were chasing the killer."

Argh's smile disappeared. "You what?"

As we joined my brother on the path, Deitz ran him through our boiler room search and the subsequent chase experience.

"Nicely done, you two. You just messed up any chance we might have had of catching the guy."

"*We* didn't do anything. *We* were just looking for Shakes and caught the suspect leaving the hotel. You're lucky we saw him at all," I argued.

Argh's shoulders twitched in the barest of shrugs. "This

investigation should have been simple. But no part of it has been easy."

"Do you think the guy already knew about that door?" Eddie asked.

My brother shrugged. "Doubtful. If he had, why would he have stuck around after killing our victim. It seems more likely that he followed you two down there. Either way, he's gone. And we're back to square one."

"And I've lost Shakes," I said, tears burning my eyes.

"Not necessarily," Eddie said. "The guy we were chasing wasn't carrying Shakes."

I thought about that. "Maybe he left Shakes in the hotel?"

Always the party pooper, Argh said, "Of course, if he's been coming and going through that boiler room door all along, he could have taken the dog out of the hotel as soon as he snagged him."

The whisper of hope Deitz had given me fled and my steps grew heavy. I walked in silence all the way back.

Shouting greeted us as we stepped into the hotel. Argh stiffened at the sound and quickly scanned the lobby, assessing the situation. Despite the level of noise, the chaos seemed limited to two people standing in front of the check-out counter, and two desk clerks behind it, trying to get them to calm down.

Well-built with pale skin and red hair, the woman seemed to be doing most of the screaming. "You don't fool me!" she shouted in response to something Peter Steel must have said. "You killed her and I know it."

I realized I recognized her. It was the woman from the restroom. The crime documenter who worked as a professional mourner on the side.

"Don't be ridiculous," Steel said. "Why would I kill Angeline?"

"Because you're a pox on society..." she went on, reaching a hand into her purse and pulling out a gun. "We'd all be better off if you were gone." The woman held the gun down by her thigh, not pointing it at Steel. But the threat was there and he'd gone very still.

The desk clerks stumbled backward, looking for a way out.

Argh glanced at Eddie and my PI nodded, moving around the ruckus with admirable speed and silence. I watched him make a wide turn and move in behind the woman as Argh took a more direct approach.

Pulling his gun, he held it down by his side so as not to escalate things unnecessarily. Still, the woman's gaze widened when she saw him holding the weapon. "Ma'am, I'm going to need you to put the gun on the floor and slide it to me with your foot."

Steel forced a smile and seemed to relax. In fact, he almost looked bored. His handsome face lit up with a care- less smile when he spotted me. "Angeline's niece. We meet again."

I gave him a repressive look and he laughed. "No worries. I'm getting used to being blamed. Just because I understand the human psyche, everybody thinks I go around killing people." He shook his head.

The woman made a noise that sounded like a growl. "You're a narcissistic, cold-hearted bas..."

"Now, now," Steel scolded with a spark of humor in his eyes. "Sticks and stones and all that."

She growled again. The gun lifted a few inches, still not pointed at anyone, but her white-knuckled grip was not comforting.

Argh moved closer, his gun leveled on her. "Ma'am, I'm going to ask you one more time..."

She turned an enraged glance to my brother. "You men all stick together, don't you? Women are just fodder for you. Playthings. We're not worth the energy it takes to feel badly when one of you uses and discards one of us." She shook her head, her gaze finding mine. For just a beat, I thought she was going to pull me into the conversation. Her eyes flashed and her lips tightened. "I'm sick to death of it. Maybe it's time somebody rid the world of predators like Steel."

"He's not worth it," I said without thinking. "Don't throw away your life," I added. "His time will come. Karma is a harsh mistress."

Her lips tightened and Steel turned a thoughtful look on me. He looked surprised.

After a beat, the woman nodded. "You're right. He's not worth it." She placed the gun on the floor and kicked it away. Argh hurried to grab it as Eddie came up behind the woman and grabbed her arms, pulling them behind her as she winced.

"I can't believe it!" a deep, male voice said from behind me. I turned to find Joshua Barnford striding toward us from the diner, a paper take-out bag in his hand. "Will this never end?"

A phone started to ring behind the desk but the two clerks were nowhere to be seen. They'd probably quit their jobs and left the building. I wouldn't blame them.

Barnford stopped next to Argh. "Detective, please escort Mr. Steel out of the hotel. I've had just about enough of him and his mind games."

Steel laughed.

But Argh had a different idea. He grabbed one of Steel's

arms and twisted it around behind his back, cuffing him too. Steel made a brief attempt at arguing, but didn't try too hard. Either he knew he was innocent and wasn't worried, or his ego wouldn't allow him to believe he'd be caught.

Argh looked at Deitz. "I'll take the Tropical room. You can have the ballroom."

Eddie nodded. I followed him and the woman across the lobby, leaving an irate Barnford in my wake.

Once inside the large lecture room, Eddie motioned to a chair and the woman sat without argument. He sat down across from her. I took a seat behind them, staying as unobtrusive as I could. "Now, Ms...?"

"Baxter," she said in the husky voice I remembered from before. "I apologize for that scene out there. I don't know what came over me."

"Do you always carry a gun?" Eddie asked.

To my surprise, she nodded easily. "I do, actually. I'm afraid I'm a victim of my chosen profession."

Eddie frowned. "Professional mourning?"

She laughed. "No. I study and document killers and criminals. I've seen and heard some pretty horrible things in my work."

"You work for the police?" Deitz asked.

"They use my work in their training. Occasionally I take speaking gigs to talk about my findings."

Deitz jotted some notes down on a small hotel pad he must have taken from his room. "How do you know Peter Steel?"

She gave a bitter laugh. "The old-fashioned way, I'm afraid."

"You had an affair?"

I blinked in surprise. I'd have thought she was way too smart for that.

"Years ago. In college. We took several classes together and went out once. For me the experience was important. He apparently didn't feel the same way. I saw him with a different girl at a party the next night." She shrugged, but I saw the tightness in the action. She wasn't over it yet.

"So, is it safe to say you dislike him?"

"More than safe. When I saw that he was going to be here, I nearly cancelled my reservation."

"Why go after him now?" I couldn't help asking. "After two days coexisting with the man, what made you turn on him now, when you were about to be free of him?"

She shook her head. "I should have turned my back on him out there. Just walked away. I knew as soon as I spoke to him it was a mistake. Hearing that smug voice. The icy disdain. I just wanted to put a bullet between his cold eyes."

"Something must have set you off," Deitz said.

"*He* did," she responded. "He knows how I felt about Angeline. He just couldn't keep himself from taking a jab at me. He felt compelled to tell me they'd slept together." She shuddered as if the very idea was too repulsive to bear.

"You and the victim were friends?" Eddie asked.

"Friends?" She laughed bitterly. "Something like that, yeah."

They'd been lovers, I realized. "You loved her?"

I said it softly enough she might have totally missed the question. But she didn't. She turned a pain-filled gaze to me, glossy with unshed tears. "Yes."

Eddie didn't look happy. I knew how he felt. How could one woman leave so much angst and pain in her wake. In that moment, I didn't much like Angeline.

"I'm sorry for your loss," I told her.

Baxter nodded, sniffling. "Thanks."

"Tell me what you know about Angeline's relationship

with Peter Steel. Witnesses have said Angeline was worried about someone who was manipulating her. Someone who had the power to ruin her career."

"He offered her a job working for him. Angeline knew he'd use the situation to try to seduce her. But she really wanted that job. Despite his many character flaws, Steel is brilliant. His company makes multi-millions a year working with law enforcement and the health and funeral industries. He's charming and creative and good at what he does." She grimaced as if the words were dirt on her tongue. "She was really torn."

"It sounds as if she succumbed to his seduction," Deitz said.

Ms. Baxter nodded. "I don't care about the sex, Detective." Eddie didn't bother to correct her on the title. "Angeline and I had an open relationship. I just didn't want her around him. Steel is a black pit of despair in a nice suit. He had a poisoning effect on Angel."

"What about Smith?" I asked.

Ms. Baxter frowned. "You don't have to be a psychologist to know that man is sick. He's been stalking Angel for nearly a year. She got a restraining order against him three months ago. It helped, but he just kept stalking her from a slightly bigger distance."

Deitz and I shared a look. I could tell by the expression on his face that he was wondering what I was. Had Argh known about the stalking?

"Did Smith ever show any signs of being violent?" my PI asked.

Baxter shrugged. "No. But his was a twisted mind. I believe he'd be capable of anything where Angel was concerned."

"Like killing her because she slept with another man?"

Or *men*, I thought, frowning over just how much "fun" Angeline had apparently had while she was at the convention.

"Definitely."

Deitz took Ms. Baxter's driver's license and told her to stay in the hotel until the police released her.

She looked irritated but didn't fight it too hard.

We went looking for Argh and found him walking Steel to the door, still cuffed.

"Hey?" I called out to my brother. "You're arresting him?"

Argh handed Steel off to the lovely Sarah and walked over to us. "What did you learn from the woman?"

Deitz handed my brother Ms. Baxter's license. "Pamela Baxter" he said. "Hates Steel because he dated and dumped her in college so anything she says about him is suspect. But we did learn she had a relationship with the victim."

"And that Steel is a misogynistic pig," I added helpfully.

Argh nodded, pocketing the license. "You told her to stay?"

Eddie nodded.

"Stay here and keep an eye on her," Argh said. "I'll run her through the system after I get Mr. Steel processed. Officer Sarah searched his room again and found something that wasn't there the first time."

I raised my brows in question. "Let me guess. The murder weapon."

"First time you've been right all week," Argh said.

I punched his arm hard enough to make him wince. "There's a good chance the weapon was planted," he went on. "But until we find out who planted it, Steel's going to sit in a jail cell."

16

The diner had reopened and was offering a limited menu since it was close to midnight. Deitz and I had been searching the hotel since returning and we were both beat. He thought we should eat something before going on.

I just wanted to keep looking.

Most of the attendees of the ruined convention had evacuated the hotel, leaving it feeling empty and abandoned. I saw only two cleaning staff on my way downstairs, and they both wore worried expressions and worked with fast, jerky movements.

"Everybody's waiting for the other shoe to drop," Eddie said as we stepped out of the elevator.

I nodded mutely, too worried and sad to even form words. Shakes had been gone for five hours. Five hours during which I had no idea if he was safe. Whether he was lost. Whether a killer had him in his grip. I silently cursed the interruption that had kept me from exchanging myself for my little dog. I knew Shakes was wily and brave. But was he a match for a human predator?

"May?"

Eddie's worried voice pulled me out of my reverie. My head jerked up. "Huh?"

"I asked if you wanted to eat in the diner, or take food up to your room?"

I shrugged. "I don't care. I'm not hungry anyway."

He stared at me for a moment, and then pulled me into a hug. "We'll find him, honey. I promise."

Sniffling, I pulled away, too jittery to be contained. "Don't make promises you can't keep."

The phone behind the counter was ringing again. I glanced at it after several rings, wondering where the employees had gone.

"Let's just eat in the diner," Deitz suggested. "If they find Shakes we'll be easy to locate." When I fixed him with a blank look, he added. "You haven't eaten all day. You'll think better if you put something into your stomach."

I nodded, my stash of hope having dwindled down to almost nothing. It felt as if we'd been looking for days. We'd searched every meeting room, office, shop, and facility the hotel had. When we'd finally decided to take a break, Pinella had offered to keep searching. She'd pulled Doug and a few remaining attendees together and they were going room-to-room on every floor looking for my dog.

I itched to be with them. But I knew Eddie was right. I'd eat something and then be back at it. If we didn't find my little furball in the hotel, I'd hit the streets and see if he'd somehow made it outside.

I was surprised to see Joshua Barnford sitting in a booth all by himself when we entered the diner. The organizer glanced up and waved when he saw us. I half-heartedly returned the wave and headed toward the back of the restaurant, not wanting to speak to him or anybody.

We slid into a booth just as Barnford appeared next to the table.

"Ms. Ferth. Mr. Deitz."

"Hello, Mr. Barnford," Eddie said. "I'm sorry about your convention."

He pursed his lips. "I'll recover. Notoriety isn't necessarily a bad thing. If we embrace it rather than try to hide from it, our next con will be even bigger than this one."

I doubted it, but I gave the guy points for positivity. "I'm surprised to see you still here," I told Barnford. "I figured you'd be long gone by now."

He shook his head. "There are lots of details to take care of. Vendors need to be cancelled, hotel contracts have to be renegotiated. I'll be here for several more days."

I nodded, not really caring. All my focus was on the dog who was more family than pet.

"Ms. Ferth. I noticed you searching the hotel today. Did you lose something? Can I help?"

A warm flush infused me, followed by a jolt of guilt for having treated him coldly. "Thanks for the offer. Someone took my dog, Shakespeare. I'm trying to find him."

Barnford frowned. "That's too bad. Why do you believe he's still in the hotel? As I recall, he's a tiny thing. He could easily be smuggled out in a suitcase or purse."

I blinked in surprise. Barnford was right. I looked at Deitz. "Security cameras."

He nodded and slipped from the booth. "Stay. Eat something. I'll call you when I have them queued up."

Though I was itching to follow, I nodded, knowing I'd be right behind him.

Barnford watched Eddie stride quickly out and frowned.

"Is something wrong?" I asked.

"What? Oh. No, sorry. I frown when I'm thinking. It's a bad habit."

"What were you thinking?" I motioned for the over-worked waitress, who was alone in the diner except for a cook. She had her hands full but she hurried over. "I'm sorry. But can I just get a muffin and a bottle of water?"

"Of course." To her credit, she was polite and kind. In her shoes, I was pretty sure I'd be cranky.

"...police. They make me nervous."

I refocused on Barnford. He was tugging on the lapels of his wrinkled suitcoat.

I nodded as if I'd heard what he said. "Eddie's not with the police," I told him, having guessed the direction of his thoughts. "He's a private investigator."

"Ah." Barnford's expression turned shrewd. "Then I needn't worry about the parking tickets I never paid in Asheville the last time I was in town?"

I laughed, though it sounded hollow.

"Can I help you find your little dog?" he asked after a moment of awkward silence.

"We've looked everywhere. I just don't know where else he might be."

"Have you looked in the suitcase vault?"

"Suitcase vault?" I asked. "What's that?"

He stood. "Follow me. It's probably unlikely he'd be in there, but if your goal is to look at the entire hotel, you should check that room too."

I followed Barnford out into the lobby and toward a door in the shadows behind the bellhops' podium.

He tried the knob and found it locked, then pulled a key card out of his pocket and used it to open the door.

I lifted my brows in question.

"Master key. They insisted I have one since I've been

working early and late and have to be in just about every part of the administrative side of the hotel."

"You can get into the guest rooms with that thing?"

He shook his head. "Of course not."

I wanted to believe him, but...

He pushed the door open and reached around the frame to flip a light switch. Light flooded a small room that was crammed with luggage of all shapes, vintages, and sizes. "Wow," I said.

He nodded. "You'd be surprised how many people leave their belongings behind. The hotel tries to get the items to their owners, but most people don't return calls."

"Don't they have addresses? Why not just send them back?"

"Aside from the cost of doing it, they were sued enough times for sending suitcases to abusive spouses or estranged relatives that they don't bother anymore."

I shook my head. "People are endlessly fascinating."

"That's one way to look at it."

I scanned him a look and he deflated. "I apologize. I'm feeling cranky today."

"You have a right," I soothed. Then, remembering why I was in the strange little room, I called out to Shakes.

Barnford walked around the room, moving suitcases and looking in corners and niches. We'd only gotten about halfway through the bags when Barnford's phone rang. He looked at the ID and straightened away from a large, rolling bag. "I need to go take this. I'll be right back."

I barely acknowledged him as I unzipped another large bag and gave it a quick search. I was pulling an ancient duffle bag closer when the room went dark and the door slammed shut.

My head shot up. "Barnford?" The room remained silent as a tomb and just as dark.

"Jeezopete!" I climbed to my feet with a groan and took a step. My foot slammed into a hard-sided bag and I stumbled, bouncing off another bag before crashing to the floor. "Ugh!" I patted my pockets for my phone, not finding it. With a frustrated groan, I realized I'd left it on the table in the diner.

I stood again, sliding a foot out in front of me until it bumped something squishy. I changed direction and found an open area, moving that way. I repeated the process until I felt the hard door under my fingers. Wrapping my hand around the knob, I turned.

But it didn't move.

I was locked inside the dark room.

Panic flared and I found myself pounding on the door with my fists, screaming Barnford's name. The heavy door seemed to absorb my screams and deaden my chances of being heard.

By the time my fists felt bruised, I realized Barnford wasn't coming back. He'd locked me into the tiny, impossibly dark room and was probably heading for Mexico at that moment.

As soon as I admitted that to myself, the memory I'd been trying to capture about Barnford came to life in my mind. The thought that I'd seen him somewhere before had niggled since we'd been introduced. But it had remained elusive until that horrible moment when I realized he'd set me up.

He was the man I'd seen that first day when I'd been racing for the elevator. He'd fought with the unseen woman, who I suspected was Angeline.

He'd also been one of the voices I'd heard when I'd been

trapped in the housekeeper's cart. Who had he been talking to? And why had they shoved me down the stairs?

As a popular event organizer in the PM industry, Barnford had the power to make Angeline's career go away if he was inclined. He'd offered her a job, and if she'd taken it, Barnford would be in a good spot to manipulate her. He was intelligent and, judging by my current predicament, ruthless.

Why had they fought? What had he wanted from Angeline? Was it the same thing everyone else seemed to want? Was he jealous?

Angeline's angry words came back to me, painful in the light of what had occurred shortly after she'd spoken them.

How dare you?

Barnford had obviously accused her of something, and she'd been insulted.

I certainly did not! Why must you always accuse me...

She'd left then. Stepped into the elevator, leaving him behind. And shortly after, Angeline had turned up dead.

"It was you all along, wasn't it?" I murmured into the darkness, feeling stupid for not having seen it before. He'd played me like a flute. And I'd been all too happy to let him blow the notes.

I sighed. It didn't matter. First things first. I needed to get out of that room.

But how?

Deitz would be looking for me. If I kept pounding on the door, he might hear it and come. Unfortunately, I had a sneaking suspicion Barnford had put me in that room because it was far away from the main sections of the hotel. The door was cast in shadow behind the big podium. Unless someone knew it was there, it was unlikely they'd find it.

But I couldn't just sit there and wait. I had to find a way

out. I crawled carefully toward the nearest luggage, searching the first bag I found with my fingers since it was too dark to see. When I found nothing useful, I moved on to the next bag and the next, looking for anything I could use to open the door.

I had no idea what I was looking for, or how I was going to use it to escape the room. But, I knew one thing for sure. Whatever I did, it wasn't going to be a quick process.

17

S norfle.

I wasn't sure how much time had passed. I'd given up trying to find something to open the door and was slumped against a soft-sided bag on the floor. I'd fallen asleep, dreaming of Shakes and Eddie. In my dream, I was inside my apartment and Shakes was scratching wildly at the door, yipping for me as Eddie tried to quiet him down, telling him I was napping and that he had to be quiet.

But the Pomeranian devil, as usual, had his own plans and he just redoubled his efforts to scratch his way through the door. I woke up smiling at his antics. A beat later, pain stabbed my chest as I remembered my dog was missing.

I shoved myself upright, blinking away hot tears, and fought a wave of self-pity. How had everything gone so horribly wrong?

Snorfle.

I was so deep into my pity party that, for a moment, the sound didn't register.

Snorfle.

I jerked fully into the present, finally recognizing what I was hearing. "Shakes?"

Snorfle, snorfle. "Yip!"

I started crawling toward the door. "Shakes? Is that you?"

"Yip! Yip! Yip! Yip! Yip!"

"Shakes," I said again, leaning my head against the door. "You're okay."

The door flew open and I fell out onto the scratchy carpet. A soft projectile slammed into me and a frantic tongue slathered my ears and neck. I lay there, crying softly as my dog tucked his quivering little body into mine, pressing tightly against me and whining in between licks. "Buddy," I said, my voice thick with tears. "You're okay."

"Are you all right?" a deep voice asked, the words clearly edged with worry.

I looked up into Eddie's handsome face and reached for him, pulling him down to me rather than sitting up to greet him. "I am now."

Deitz wrapped his arms around me, pulling me close. "You're going to be the death of me," he said on a sigh.

The three of us stayed that way for a long moment, only breaking apart at the sound of my brother barking orders across the lobby.

Eddie lifted his head. "She's here!"

The barking of orders ceased and the sound of fast, heavy footsteps approached. A moment later, Argh looked down at us. "Why are you laying on the floor?"

I shook my head, dragging a hand over my wet face.

Eddie took my hand and helped me sit up, handing me my phone. "I found this in The Diner."

"Thanks. Where was Shakes?"

"An elderly woman who lives across the pond found him in her garden," Argh explained. "She's been calling the hotel for hours, apparently, trying to see if he belonged to someone here, but the staff has been too preoccupied and busy to answer the phone. Officer Sarah finally answered the phone because she couldn't take it anymore."

I made a mental note to thank the lovely Sarah and a promise to myself to make it up to her for all the evil thoughts I'd had about her.

"Somebody must have let him outside, Eddie said. "Probably hoping he'd run away."

Well, I thought, It could have been worse. Much worse. I buried my face in Shakes' sweet-smelling fur and inhaled deeply. "I can't believe he's back safe."

Deitz leaned in and kissed the top of my head. "I can't believe you're safe. How'd you get into that room? If Shakes hadn't found you, we might never have. Nobody seemed to know this room was back here."

"Barnford knew it was here," I said, then frowned. "I think he's our killer. He locked me in there. He's probably halfway to Mexico by now."

Deitz and Argh shared a look.

"What?" I asked, feeling the first niggles of doubt snaking through me.

"We found Barnford outside in the bushes," Argh told me. "He'd been clocked in the head and was unconscious. If he was the one to lock you in here, he's one very unlucky guy to be attacked outside the hotel just as he was making his escape."

"Sweet Carolina!" I exclaimed. "What in the world is going on?"

"I have no idea," my brother said. He punctuated the admission with a gust of frustrated air. "But, I'm pretty sick of this case."

That made four of us, if I included Shakes. And of course I did.

"Dude!"

I turned to find Doug and Pinella hurrying toward us. Doug appeared slightly bleary-eyed. He was munching chips from a party-sized bag and had a literal air of medicinal pot around him. I imagined him walking around in a cloud of it, like Pigpen in the Peanuts® cartoons. "Where you been?" he asked in a slightly slurry voice.

"We've been lookin' all over, dolly." Pinella looked worried. "We thought you left without tellin' us."

"I'm fine," I assured them, accepting a hug from Pinella. "Barnford locked me in the suitcase vault."

"The what?" Pinella asked, frowning.

"Dude?"

I shook my head. "Not important. I'm just relieved Shakes is back." I looked at Argh. "Can we go home now?"

He nodded. "That's probably best."

Relief slid through me. "Is everybody else gone?"

"Most people have left. I think a couple of the attendees decided to stay and enjoy Asheville," Eddie told me. "But I wouldn't be surprised if they switched hotels. The Mountain View Conference Center is functioning on a bare bones staff. It's not a happy place to be right now."

I felt bad for the hotel. "Hopefully, this won't affect their ongoing business."

Eddie shrugged. "Give it a few weeks and people will be frothing at the bit to come see the spot where the people were shot at or stabbed."

Argh nodded. "I see a thriller writer's convention in the hotel's near future."

I laughed. "You're probably right."

A familiar, stiffly arrogant figure came through the front door and I tensed.

Argh sighed. "I'll go fill our DIC in on the latest developments."

"If Robard's the detective in charge, why have you been doing all the work on this?"

"Good question," Argh said, lifting a hand to catch the other detective's attention. "Apparently he was too busy to deal with it. And since my sister was involved, he figured I'd be fine with taking charge."

"Handy," I said, frowning. "What do you want to bet he'll be right there when the kudos are handed out."

Argh snorted out a laugh and strode toward the sour-faced police detective waiting by the door.

Robard made an "I'm watching you" motion and I gave it back. He laughed.

"Shall we go home?" Deitz asked. I nodded. "I can have my stuff packed in five minutes."

He narrowed his gaze on me. "Five minutes? I saw how many clothes you brought. There's no way you'll be done that fast."

Gathering Shakes close and kissing him on his tiny, soft head, I turned toward the elevator. "For your information, I only unpacked a few things." If two dozen pairs of shoes counted as a few. "I'll bet you dinner at The Burger Bar that I'll beat you back to the lobby."

He hurried past me with a grin. "You're on."

I tried to run to catch up, but Shakes gave a yip of displeasure that I was bobbling him. I put him on the floor and made kissy noises for him to follow when I took off running.

"No running in the lobby," a familiar, crabby voice called out. I flipped a dismissive hand toward Robard and slowed to a race walk. Shakes and I hit one elevator just as Deitz hit the other. I bounced on my toes as the door slowly closed. "He'll have an advantage on us," I told Shakes. My dog sneezed and gave me his best doggy grin. "He's on the fourth floor. I'll have to make up time in packing and take the stairs if we're going to beat him."

Shakes' back end wriggled with excitement. He was always up for an adventure.

After what felt like hours, the door opened on the fifth floor and I surged out, my thumbs busily typing a text to Argh, instructing him to waylay Eddie on the fourth floor and keep him there as long as he could. I told him there was a double cheeseburger combo plate in it for him. That would catch his interest.

Shakes gave a yip of surprise as a woman appeared in front of the doors. I just barely kept from running over Pamela Baxter as I surged out of the car.

Baxter yelped in surprise.

"Oh!" I said. "I'm sorry." I started around her, but she stopped me with a hand on my arm.

Shakes growled, clearly not interested in any more shenanigans.

"Shh, buddy," I scolded.

Pamela yanked her hand away, looking sheepish. "Sorry. The little guy's really protective of you, isn't he?"

"He is. Plus, we've had a tough couple of days." I glanced at my phone, seeing I'd wasted a full minute already. "I'm sorry. I really need to go."

Pamela nodded. "Could you just suggest a good place to have dinner?"

I groaned internally, then quickly listed several favorites of mine and Deitz's. "You can't go wrong with any of them." I tried to surreptitiously glance at my watch again. "I really need to go..."

She smiled. "What's the hurry?"

I wanted to scream. The woman must be lonely. As soon as I had the thought, I felt guilty. Of course she was feeling bereft. She'd lost someone she'd cared about in the most horrible way. Giving an internal sigh, I smiled back. "Just a dumb bet with Eddie. It's not important." I'd just have to dip into my savings to buy him his customary three burgers and two fries. But he was buying the ice cream afterward. That thought made me feel better.

"Ah. Eddie's a cop, right?"

Something about the way her gaze sharpened engaged my spidey senses. "He's a private investigator. My brother's a detective with the Hillside PD. My dad's a Lieutenant." Shakes circled my feet, his tail high and wagging fast. Something was stressing him out.

I glanced around, looking for trouble. "I really should go. We're checking out." I gave Baxter another smile, hoping to take some of the tightness from her pale features. "Are you leaving soon?"

"Not soon, no. I have something I need to do first."

"Oh, okay. Well. It was really nice meeting you," I said, offering her my hand. "Maybe we'll see each other again at the next con."

Pamela wasn't paying attention. She frowned toward the door at the end of the hall, near the elevators.

"Pamela?"

The woman blinked and looked at me. "Sorry. I was just..." She bit her bottom lip. "That was Angeline's room. She was complaining about the elevator noise the night before she..."

Down by my feet, Shakes vibrated under a nearly silent growl. His tiny lip curled, showing small, white teeth.

"She thought I was calling to check up on her." Baxter shook her head. "I wasn't. But *he* was there. And I suddenly couldn't stand it."

My spidey senses shot into overdrive. I took a step back and tried to surreptitiously dial Argh. Unfortunately, I wasn't sneaky enough.

A pale fist shot out and slammed into my throat and I went down as if I'd been shot, fighting to catch my breath.

18

Agony flared into alarm as I fought to breathe through my panic. I knew about throat injuries... about the danger of a crushed larynx. One of Argh's friends had taken an elbow to the throat during a football game in high school and the kid had almost died.

I felt as if I was dying. The pain was excruciating, and I was starting to feel dizzy from lack of air.

On some level, I was aware of Shakes dancing all over me. He was snarling and lunging at someone, and there were screams. I knew I needed to snap out of it. To protect him.

But the pain.

In sheer desperation, I sucked in a quick breath and finally realized I wasn't going to die. Not from the throat punch, anyway. A moment later, the dizziness improved, and my thoughts cleared enough to realize Pamela Baxter had a knife and she was trying to use it on me. Or Shakes. I wasn't sure which of us was her target. Maybe both.

All I knew for sure was that she would have already

gotten me if my dog weren't there. I grabbed Shakes around the middle and scooted away, looking for my phone.

It was on the ground near the elevator, too far away to grab.

Baxter stepped closer. "You shouldn't have stuck your nose in," she told me. "You should have left well enough alone. But every time I turned around, there you were, getting all up in my grill."

I swallowed and fire filled my throat. I was going to have to give up swallowing for a while. I tried to focus on what she was saying, the task made more difficult by the fact that my dog kept trying to eat her.

I tugged Shakes closer, wrapping an arm around his tiny chest so he couldn't escape. When I managed to speak, the words came out broken. "I wasn't in your grill." I swallowed and immediately wished I hadn't. "I was just trying to help."

She curled one shapely lip, giving Shakes a run for his money. "I told her not to come to this stupid convention. I told her I didn't like her being here without me. But she insisted. She didn't want to be exclusive." Baxter's face was nearly purple with rage. "She didn't want to be tied down by anything."

I realized my only hope was to keep her talking. Maybe Deitz would come looking for me if enough time passed. "I heard you talking on the phone that night," I said, my mind finally putting all the pieces together. "You'd accused her of something. She'd sounded unhappy."

Baxter snorted. "Unhappy? Hardly. She had everything she wanted."

"What was that?" I asked, fighting to keep my gaze from sliding longingly to the elevator.

Baxter moved closer, the knife far too close for comfort.

"One of them was with her, wasn't he? I could hear him whispering to her. The idiot apparently thought I was deaf as well as dumb." She sounded so bitter, yet so sad at the same time.

"You came to talk to her and found her with Barnford."

Baxter's gaze turned hard at mention of the organizer's name. "He'd promised her a partnership. Did you know that?"

I shook my head, getting my feet underneath me and bracing one hand so I could jump to my feet more quickly. I just needed to get Shakes and me to my room. I just...

There was no way I'd get the door open before that knife was at my throat. I'd have to find another way.

I assessed my options in the hallway. There weren't many. Down the hall was a room-service tray filled with half-eaten food. I might find a fork or knife there, but neither would be any match for her blade, which looked to be six inches long and very sharp.

Behind her were two upholstered chairs, too bulky for me to throw. There was a metal lamp on the table between the chairs, if I could get to it.

"Besides," Baxter went on. "Barnford wasn't my concern. He's weak. Easily cowed. It was the other one." She actually growled when she said, "other one".

"Who's that?" I asked, tensing my muscles to rise.

"Steel. He's the real monster. That man's a pig. He's left more broken hearts behind him than a funeral home."

Something clicked in my mind. "Is that why you confronted him in the lobby? Right in front of the police?"

She grinned, her expression coldly amused. "I needed them to search his room again. Otherwise, planting that knife would have been a wasted effort. I hate to waste my time and energy."

I lifted a fraction of an inch off the carpet, digging the toes of my sneakers into the floor. "You wanted him blamed for everything."

"I did. There was a certain pleasant irony behind him finally going to prison for something he didn't do. I adore good irony. Don't you?"

"Sometimes," I said, stalling. "And Smith? What did he have to do with this?"

She grinned, clearly proud of herself. "That was a fun interlude, wasn't it? Calling him was a stroke of genius, don't you think? All he needed to hear was that Steel was seducing Angeline against her will and he was off like a ballistic missile. But Barnford was the most fun. Telling him you were on to him. Convincing him to shove you down the steps in that cart." She laughed as if someone had told her a great joke. "Poor Barnford has some skeletons in his closet. I'm afraid his guilt makes him easy to manipulate. He didn't even question me when I asked him to meet me outside the hotel tonight." Her grin was mean.

"Why'd you hit him?"

She shrugged. "It was only a matter of time until he talked to the cops. Idiot thought it was his best option for avoiding a murder charge."

I realized at that moment she'd orchestrated my getting locked into the suitcase vault, whether it had been her who'd actually done it, or if she'd told Barnford to turn the lock, it didn't matter. "This has all been a game to you, hasn't it? Creating the fake blood trail. Spiking the punch to corrupt our viewing for Angeline. Manipulating everyone into position and watching the fireworks play out."

"A game. Yes," she said, her grin growing wider. "Every step of the way. She made a little pouty face. "Did you miss your little dog?"

Shakes' growl grew louder. I scratched the back of his neck to soothe him.

"You took him." I said. Not a question. "You wanted to throw me off balance. You didn't really need me to get you out of the hotel, did you?"

Instead of answering me, she asked her own question. "Do you remember the blueprint killer? He'd lure people into large buildings that had hidden doors and secret passageways only he knew about. Then he'd stalk and terrorize them for hours before killing them. I thought that sounded like such fun. I've been coming and going the whole time and nobody knew it."

The woman was truly demented.

"You have to admit, I didn't hurt the little guy though," she said, nodding toward Shakes. "I love animals. Angeline and I had that in common. I just set him free and he wandered happily away." She frowned down at my enraged dog. "Too bad he came back. I guess I'm going to have to hurt him after all."

I released Shakes and shoved to my feet.

Baxter lunged, the blade slicing a shallow cut in my palm as I instinctively lifted it to ward off her attack. Pain burned across my skin and I knew I had to move. Shakes lunged at her, snarling, and I used the distraction to dodge past her and reach for the lamp. She came at me with a feral scream, the knife lifted above her head.

Shakes' jaw clamped over the back of her ankle and she screamed in agony, trying to shake him off.

Somehow he held on. But she was turning, the knife sliding toward him. I panicked, yanked the lamp hard enough to unplug it from the wall and swung as hard as I could. The metal base hit her in the arm and the knife went flying. It hit the stairwell door, clattering loudly against the metal frame, and slid to the ground.

"Shakes!" I yelled, and he released her ankle.

Baxter growled her rage and turned, flinging herself at me and wrapping her fingers around my throat. She was a strong woman and I thought she was going to kill me. With her fingers wrapped around my throat, I couldn't miss the "Love" tattoo on her wrist that matched the one on Angeline's ankle. At the moment, Baxter seemed a little short on love and pretty high on rage.

I kneed her hard, aiming for her belly. Missing, I got her thigh. She grunted in pain but held on to me, adrenaline making her nearly immune to pain.

Shakes locked onto Baxter's other ankle, whipping his head from side to side in an effort to get her off me.

My arms flailed, clawing at her face and punching ineffectually at her throat.

Despite Shakes' and my best efforts, my world was going charcoal around the edges. I needed to breathe, and my already bruised throat was in agony. I had maybe ten seconds before I became helpless.

I couldn't let that happen.

My brain formed a solution. It was a stupid solution, but it was all I had. I was nearly too weak to make it happen. If I was going to have any chance...it would have to happen fast.

Without further thought, I grabbed her shirt in both hands and let my weight drop. The sudden change in weight distribution made her stumble forward. Folding my legs, I allowed myself to fall back, yanking her down with me.

Baxter plunged downward, her head slamming into the heavy wooden table with a meaty thunk. To my relief, she went limp.

Unfortunately, she went heavy too. Gasping for breath, I was fighting to get her off me when the elevator doors opened and Eddie walked out. He stood staring at me for a beat, looking flabbergasted. Then he seemed to realize what he was seeing and hurried forward.

He yanked Baxter sideways and she rolled off me, hitting the carpet like a bloody ragdoll. "What in the world, May?" he asked, helping me sit up. Then he frowned, his finger running gently over my bruised throat. "Baxter did this?"

I nodded, tears finally falling as the reality of what had just happened slid over me.

Deitz fussed over me for a few minutes, cataloguing my injuries and trying to talk me into a trip to the hospital. I refused and he finally gave up. But I could tell the argument wasn't over. He seldom gave in that easily.

Shakes trotted over and fixed his button gaze accusingly on Deitz, his tail drooping.

"Hey, Cujo," Deitz said, "Sorry I'm late to the party."

Shakes yipped unhappily. Eddie jerked his head toward Baxter's bloody ankles. "I'm guessing he did that?"

I nodded.

He fixed me with a speculative look. "Your throat's sore?" I nodded again. He leaned close and kissed me gently on the lips. "How about we skip burgers and just have ice cream."

I closed my eyes in pure bliss. Ice cream would feel amazing on my sore throat.

"Let me call Argh and you can tell us what happened. Then we can go get you a medicinal vanilla shake. After that, just a quick trip to the ER."

I opened my mouth to argue, then gave up with a sigh. He was right. I should have my throat looked at.

Undaunted by talk of ERs and doctors, my little devil barked happily. Some might suggest it was because Deitz had said "shake", a word very like his own name. But I knew better. The Pomeranian devil understood what shake meant. It meant ice cream.

It meant pup cup.

And the Pomeranian devil was all about the pup cup.

19

I opened my mouth and croaked out a few words. My voice came out as a broken whisper and felt like blades slicing my throat. Argh and Robard stared at me as I tried to speak. I'd typed out my statement the day before, but the two cops had a few more questions for me.

I shook my head to let them know it wasn't going to happen.

"She's not supposed to use her voice," Eddie said, scowling at the two men. "Why don't you ask her Yes and No questions so she can just shake her head?"

Argh agreed, probably not wanting to face the wrath of the Lieutenant if he caused me to damage my throat even more than it already was. Robard scowled back at Deitz, clearly thinking I was faking my injury.

I pointed to my tablet, lifting my brows.

Robard was noticeably put out, but nodded. "If that's the best you can do."

I grabbed it, wincing as the movement pulled at the cut on my palm, and settled in, giving them an expectant look.

"First," Argh said, "I'll tell you what we learned about Pamela Baxter."

I nodded.

"As you know, she had a relationship with Angeline Porter."

I nodded again.

"From what we've been able to learn, the victim viewed Pamela Baxter as a good friend, nothing more. Yet Baxter had developed an unhealthy obsession with Porter."

I frowned.

"Baxter didn't want Porter to come to Mourning Con but she insisted. So, although Baxter wasn't registered for the event, she came and watched Porter from afar."

I typed a question and showed it to Argh.

He read it aloud for the others. "Was Baxter what she said she was? A behaviorist? Author? Worked with the police?" He nodded. "She was. Which explained her deep knowledge of crime and criminal behavior."

Robard blew air through his lips. He stood with his beefy arms crossed over his chest, his legs wide. His stance screamed irritation and aggression. I lifted my brows in question. "None of that is important now," he said, not bothering to hide his impatience. "Let's talk about what matters."

Argh ignored him. "While at the con, Angeline did what Angeline apparently always did. She partied. With everyone."

"And Baxter didn't like what she saw," Deitz offered, nodding.

"She did not. That fight you heard at the elevators," Argh said, looking at me. "That was Pamela Baxter accusing Angeline Porter of getting too friendly with too many people."

I typed a single word with a question mark. *Barnford?*

"As you suspected, he was there," Robard said, finally relenting. "Baxter saw them together and assumed the worst. But, as far as we can tell, he and Porter weren't lovers. Apparently, Barnford pitched a job offer to Angeline. He considered her a natural for event coordination. She was a people person. Friendly."

"Too friendly," Argh said, frowning. "Baxter talked Porter into meeting her in the large lecture room that night. They fought and Baxter killed Porter."

I remembered the conversation I'd had with Pamela Baxter about knives and women killers. She'd used that knowledge to throw suspicion to someone else. I typed my observation out, letting the two cops read it.

Robard nodded. "She's smart. And she was right. I never guessed our killer was a woman because of her weapon choices. Both stabbing and strangulation are generally favored by male killers."

My fingers flew over the keys. *She was with Barnford when they shoved me down the stairs in the cart?*

Robard's lips twitched and I glared at him.

He lifted his hands in surrender. "Sorry, I'm just picturing you and the laundry bumping down the stairs." He shook his head. "I can't believe you thought it was two guys. Couldn't you tell by the voice that one was a chick?"

I gave him a look for the "chick" reference and then typed my response, holding it up for him to see. *She has a deep voice and was whispering. Impossible to tell. Especially with towels on my head.*

Robard laughed.

Argh narrowed his gaze on the other cop. "In answer to your question, that was her, yes, and Barnford. Apparently she convinced him that you were trying to pin the murder on him. He'd had a previous issue with a female associate and she'd ended up dead. There's no evidence Barnford was responsible in any way for the woman's death, but if he became a suspect in Porter's murder..."

"All that old news would be dug up," Argh finished for him. "According to Barnford, they didn't intend to kill you with the cart escapade. But, when they realized you'd heard them talking, Baxter panicked and gave you a shove. Barnford claims he felt bad about it later."

I made a face.

Argh nodded his agreement. "I didn't believe him either. But he did change his story a bit later and claim they were only trying to scare you off."

Deitz chuckled. "They don't know her very well, do they?"

Argh snorted out a laugh.

Ignoring them, I typed, *Smith?*

Robard glared at me. "We're supposed to be getting information from *you*," he complained. "Not the other way around."

I shrugged.

"The would-be fiancé," Argh said. "As Baxter told you, she called Smith and fed him a line that made him come rushing over with murder in his heart. But there's no evidence that Angeline was actually engaged to Smith. Apparently, she just liked the lavish gifts he kept giving her. Like those massive diamond earrings she was wearing when she was killed," he said. "

Sounds like Baxter knew her pretty well, I typed.

"Not as well as she thought," Robard snarked.

"So, what questions did you have for May?" Eddie asked. He sat down on the couch next to me, his nearness feeling like protection. I clasped his hand in mine as Shakes jumped up on the couch and stretched out between us, his tiny nose on my leg. Tears burned as I realized how blessed I was.

Angeline Porter had caused no end of hurt feelings trying to live her life the way she wanted. Though her actions had often been thoughtless and self-centered, an argument could be made that she had a right to live as she liked. She'd drawn a lot of negativity her way with her actions. And it made me sad that, in the end, she'd died alone and terrified.

"It's about Jessie Marks," Argh said. "We can't figure out the motive for his attack. We know he and the victim had a fling. At first, we assumed that was why Baxter tried to kill him..."

"But she didn't try to kill Peter Steel, even though she had an old grudge against him, or Barnford," Eddie finished for him. He shook his head. "Can't you ask him why?"

"He won't talk about it," Robard said with a frown. "Says it doesn't matter. Angeline is dead either way."

"The man's an emotional wreck," Argh told us. "He just stares out the window of his room in the hospital." My brother's expression lightened suddenly. "By the way," he told me, "Baxter has a large bruise over her ribs. Marks was right that he'd hurt his attacker. That helps us pin his attack on her, if nothing else."

I nodded, oddly pleased that Marks had gotten a little bit of payback for what Pamela Baxter had done to him.

"Any idea what the attack might have been about?" Argh asked me.

I nodded, because I'd been giving that some thought. My fingers flew across the keyboard. A minute later, I presented my speculation: *I'm guessing that Baxter saw Marks barge into the faux viewing, clearly angry. She was probably intrigued by his standing up for Angeline and curious about the reason for it.*

Knowing Jessie, he probably told Baxter he was in love with Angeline and in Baxter's chaotic mental state, it was enough to set her off. Jessie Marks is the kind of guy a woman like Angeline might fall for if she got tired of playing around. Baxter might have felt threatened by him. Whatever the reason, I'm guessing she struck up a conversation and drew him away.

Robard frowned.

"If that's true," Argh said, clearly trying to think it through. "How'd she get him into the garden room? Marks is a big guy. Baxter probably only weighs a hundred and thirty pounds."

I held up a finger and typed out a theory: *She didn't have to drag him. He probably walked down there with her voluntarily. Maybe he was enjoying discussing Angeline with someone who knew and loved her. Remember, the blood trail was false. The only real blood was the handprint on the glass. That probably happened after Baxter attacked him. Now that I know it was Baxter, I realize why she created the false trail like that. She wrote about criminals and their methods. She mentioned Dwight Crocker Maynard to me. Remember him?*

The cops nodded. Eddie grimaced. "Sick jerk."

I nodded my agreement, and went on: *You're right, Baxter is smart. And she likes to think she's clever too.* I recognized that trait in her because I shared it. A key part of what made me a good actress was my ability to read people. And I'd read Baxter well enough to know she'd enjoy trying to put one over on others. *She talked about how Maynard studied people and used their biases and tendencies against them. She mentioned the campers whom Maynard had drawn into the woods with a fake blood trail...*

Robard perked up. "Ah. I remember. Maynard assumed the couple would investigate the trail themselves because they were fascinated by real crime and law enforcement,"

He said before eyeing me. "I'm guessing she thought you'd be nosy too?"

She wanted me to find him. Either she hoped to throw suspicion in another direction, or she never intended for Marks to die. I shrugged. *Baxter thought she was clever. She liked playing mental games. Everything she did over the last couple of days was to create chaos and confusion. She was messing with us.*

"I wondered why the hesitation knife marks," Argh said. "She had no hesitation with the victim. Maybe you're right. Maybe she didn't want him to die."

"Or there was no passion in the attack as there'd been with Porter," Robard added.

Whatever the reason, I went on. *It reminded me that I overhead one of the actors complaining his prop bag was missing. I'm betting there was fake blood in that bag.*

Deitz perked up. "Could she have disguised herself to look like a man? Like the cop Pinella thought she saw on the back stairs?"

I nodded. *She was an actress as well as a criminal behavioral scientist. If I'd thought about that combination of skills for five minutes, I probably would have guessed she was our killer.*

We sat in silence for a beat, considering everything we knew, and then Deitz asked, "Do we assume Baxter was the shooter too?"

"She admitted to the shooting, yes," Argh said. "She was trying to get us to send everybody home. And, though she lives in Indiana and we would have told her not to leave North Carolina, she would have likely driven home anyway. I'm sure she never expected that we'd figure out it was her."

"Given her work, she had a lot of good teachers on how to get away with murder," Eddie said. "Now that I know it was her who attacked me in May's room, I realize my attacker was on the small side to be a man."

What about the back stairs from the restaurants? I typed. *How'd she know about them?*

"Baxter put herself through college waitressing," Argh said. "She'd visited with the waitstaff at dinner the night before, forming a relationship built on shared experiences. I'm guessing she asked them how they delivered food without being jostled and abused by the attendees."

Smart, I thought. The woman had definitely learned a lot from the criminals she studied.

To my vast relief, the two cops left a few minutes later and I collapsed on the couch. Shakes stretched out beside me, burrowing under the soft, knitted throw Eddie had draped over me. "Are you hungry?" he asked.

I shook my head, pointing to my throat. Eating hurt too much. "I got you chocolate pudding," he coaxed.

My eyes went wide and I nodded.

Chuckling, Eddie kissed the top of my head and went into the kitchen. "The Lieutenant called. He'll be here later to check on you."

I deflated. The last thing I needed was to be lectured for an hour over getting myself embroiled in another murder investigation.

Eddie arrived with a big bowl of pudding. He handed it to me, his other hand behind his back. The blanket rose and quivered as the Pomeranian Devil worked his way out from under it. He fixed Deitz with a hopeful look and my boyfriend grinned. "No chocolate for you, little man. It's toxic for furry heroes."

Shakes drooped, looking dejected.

Eddie showed my dejected dog his other hand. It held a tiny bowl containing vanilla pudding.

Shakes yipped with excitement, his tail whipping the air behind him. He dove in as soon as Eddie gave it to him.

"I can't believe he thought I'd forget him." Eddie sounded so hurt, I had to grin. He eased down next to me, careful not to dislodge our treats. "By the way, I meant to warn you..."

He didn't get a chance to finish that sentence. The doorbell rang and he sighed. "I guess it's too late for a warning."

I set my pudding down with a feeling of dread, fighting the instinct to run back to my room and hide. When the door opened, I realized my instinct had been a good one.

"Dude!" Doug said, his arms filled with bags and boxes. "I come bearing goodies."

Pinella scooted through the door behind him, a casserole dish in her hotmitt-covered hands. "Hey, Dolly. We brought you a party so you wouldn't be bored."

I rolled my lips to hide a smile, and scanned Eddie a look.

He was grinning. "I told them it was a great idea to come cheer you up." He lifted his brows as I forced a smile. "Oh good. I'm so happy," I whispered.

Doug handed the food bags to Deitz. "I'll keep the box. This is the heart of the party right here."

I couldn't wait to see what he'd brought. If only to have the horror story building in my head realized.

Pinella followed Eddie into the kitchen, returning a minute later. "We brought all soft foods," she assured me. "Ice cream, chicken velvet soup, shrimp fettuccini, pancakes, deviled eggs and crustless pumpkin pie."

My mouth watered.

"Also, a variety of hot teas with lemon and honey," Doug said as he sat down and started sorting through his box. He extracted *Love Actually* from the box, which was my favorite chick flick of all time, and two other movies I loved, along with a Charades game and scrabble.

Doug started the movie and handed me the remote. "Sit. Stay. We'll bring the food to you."

I leaned back with a grin and pulled Shakes onto my lap. The little dog had finished his pudding and was eyeing mine. I picked it up and made short work of what was left so he couldn't get it. Shakes' tail drooped with disappointment.

Until the food-laden trays started to arrive.

I was pretty sure I'd died and gone to heaven.

Later, when our bellies were full and Shakes lay stretched out next to me, Eddie snuggled into my other side, and Pinella and Doug bickering over which of them had brought the best soft food, I knew life was back to its happy normal.

And noisy though it was, I wouldn't have it any other way.

The End

DON'T MISS OUT

Stay up on all Sam's news by joining her newsletter, and get a copy of a fun mystery just for signing up!

SIGN UP HERE!
https://samcheever.com/newsletter/

READ MORE GRAVE THEATRICS

Book 1: Grave Theatrics

It's definitely curtains for May's client. He's exited Stage Left for the last time.

May Ferth just wants to do a good job in her role as a fake girlfriend. But there are strange goings-on at the funeral. Shifty characters whispering secrets in shadowed corners and a truly yummy advocate for the dead guy implying that May might have had something to do with his friend's unscripted exit.

May might be a thirty-three-year-old ex-community theater actress on her second career, but she comes from a family of cops. And, despite her talent for acting, she has a lot more Detective in her than Diva.

The villain thinks he can threaten her and she'll fold like last week's panned play. Clearly, he hasn't read the day's script changes. May and her little dog Shakespeare are on the case. Though, they might take a little direction from the

Private Investigator who believes that May's client was murdered and fully intends to prove it.

Read more books in this fun series: https://samcheever.com/books/#grave

ABOUT THE AUTHOR

USA Today and Wall Street Journal Bestselling Author Sam Cheever writes mystery and suspense, creating stories that draw you in and keep you eagerly turning pages. Known for writing great characters, snappy dialogue, and unique and exhilarating stories, Sam is the award-winning author of 100+ books.

To learn more about Sam and her work, visit her at one of her online hotspots:
www.samcheever.com
samcheever@samcheever.com

ALSO BY SAM CHEEVER

If you enjoyed **An Unconventional Mourning**, you might also enjoy these other fun series by Sam. To find out more, visit the **BOOKS** page at www.samcheever.com:

Grave Theatrics Mysteries - For more fun with May and Shakespeare

Country Cousin Mysteries

Silver Hills Cozy Mysteries

Gainfully Employed Mysteries

Midlife Muddle Paranormal Women's Fiction

Mature Magic Paranormal Women's Fiction

Enchanting Inquiries Paranormal Cozy Mysteries

Yesterday's Paranormal Mysteries

Reluctant Familiar Paranormal Mysteries

Honeybun Heat Series